Braver's real achievement here is his brilliant exploration of the nature of art, accident, and truth, and how it's the hardest moral choices we are forced to make that determine, in the end, who and what we are.

—Sigrid Nunez, author of National Book Award Winner *The Friend*

Braver's novel is rich and humane, a tightly controlled, beautifully orchestrated portrait of contemporary terrors and the feedback loops of fear and paranoia they create that mesmerize us and, tragically, sometimes drive us mad. There are those that disappear in the violence, and those that disappear searching for them in their wakes, trying to make sense of insanity.

—Paul Harding, winner of the Pulitzer Prize

It is both profoundly personal and smartly political, a memorable page turner with urgent, resonant themes.

—Alix Ohlin, author of *Signs and Wonder*

Adam Braver has written a brilliant, disturbingly bold, beautiful novel . . . Reading it provides unforeseen, indispensable rewards.

—Howard Norman, author of *The Bird Artist*

Adam Braver has a wonderfully rich imagination and his grasp of historical characters and settings is both deep and natural. I would gladly read anything he writes.

—Dan Chaon, author of the National Book Award Finalist
Among the Missing

Absolutely contemporary, with all the pith and confusion of events still in motion. —Stewart O'Nan, author of *Snow Angels*

Adam Braver has pulled off quite a feat, realigning all our notions and expectations of historical fiction.

—Phillip Lopate, author of *Portrait of My Body*

Rejoice the Head of Paul McCartney

a novel

Adam Braver

Cover and book design by Alex Dimeff.

Library of Congress Cataloging-in-Publication Data

Names: Braver, Adam, 1963- author.
Title: Rejoice the head of Paul McCartney : a novel / Adam Braver.
Description: New Orleans, Louisiana : University of New Orleans Press,
   [2022]
Identifiers: LCCN 2022028871 (print) | LCCN 2022028872 (ebook) | ISBN
   9781608012411 (paperback ; acid-free paper) | ISBN 9781608012886 (ebook)

Subjects: LCGFT: Novels.
Classification: LCC PS3602.R39 R45 2022 (print) | LCC PS3602.R39 (ebook)
   | DDC 813/.6--dc23/eng/20220617
LC record available at https://lccn.loc.gov/2022028871
LC ebook record available at https://lccn.loc.gov/2022028872

Selections have been published previously in *The Normal School*
and *Action, Spectacle*.

This is a work of fiction. Names, characters, places, and incidents are
the product of the author's imagination or are used fictitiously.

Printed in the United States of America on acid-free paper.

UNIVERSITY OF NEW ORLEANS PRESS
2000 Lakeshore Drive
New Orleans, Louisiana 70148
unopress.org

In memory of my mother.
Most remembered, some forgotten.

The Billboard

i.

IN DECEMBER of 1969, a billboard on the Sunset Strip advertised the album *Abbey Road*. Giant Beatles strolled across the crosswalk, the tops of their heads cut out and extending above the panels. They surveyed the border of West Hollywood, just below the famed Chateau Marmont, and although the picture was taken on Abbey Road, it was as if they were strolling across Sunset Boulevard: John in white, Ringo in black, George in denim, and a cigarette dangling Paul with his feet bare. Their heads rose just above the top of the canvas, in the skies over Los Angeles.

People stopped to take pictures. Stared at it as if it wasn't advertising but as though it had personality, and, in its own way, was a living part of the cultural landscape. It was a welcome distraction from Nixon, politics, racial injustice, the draft, and the war itself. But not long after the billboard had appeared, someone had climbed up the scaffold, cut away Paul McCartney's head, and stolen it. The headless Paul made an eerie sight for those few days that the billboard remained up, transformed into an ominous reminder of the times we were living in.

"One more tear in the fabric," said the woman who would become my wife.

We were stopped in traffic on Sunset, just below the billboard and the decapitated McCartney. It was the usual backup, enhanced by cars slowing to gawk at the sign. A teenager wearing a thin leather headband stumbled up the sidewalk, wasted. It wasn't even noon. We were hardly much older than him, and

yet it felt as though we'd crossed a line. I had just started a temporary job for the State of California that would end up lasting
for decades, and the woman who would become my wife, a social
worker for the County, dealt with kids like him all the time who
called her *ma'am*. Sometimes we wondered how it was that we'd
already aged out.

She pointed up at the billboard. "You know, if you squint, it's
like the sun is making a halo where his head was."

Traffic still wouldn't budge.

I said, "Maybe he blew his mind out in a car."

She accused me of always having to make a joke. And then
she said the thing about the *tear in the fabric* again, her go-to line
for how anything bad that happened in the world was subvert-
ing our destiny of being a good and peaceful society. I suggested
that maybe there was another way to look at it. Perhaps the
world was naturally torn, a collection of frayed patches barely
held together.

"Maybe," I said, "it is a negative effect, that, in fact, you're
only noticing the space between the tears and not the tears themselves."

"Now you're just being intentionally obtuse."

"I'm only saying, maybe this isn't a tear at all. Maybe it's the
tears that let the light in."

She shook her head. "It's okay," she said. "Never mind."

The traffic broke, and we motored off, not talking for the rest
of the drive.

The billboard came down within a week. The authorities
hadn't found the Paul McCartney head, concluding it had been
spirited off to the hills and then to who knows where in the valley.
By that time, it was something we'd hoped to have long forgotten.

ii.

The way Monty was found was unimaginable—on a back stoop
in an alley, his arms looped around the railings. The pose was

almost religious. There were no suspects. No known motive. It was beyond any of our comprehension, do-good college students, who, in our efforts to end the war, had, until then, imagined ourselves on the outskirts of the law.

This was a whole different level.

Between having been on the go-kart circuit and having had a side business as a small-time drug dealer, there was a time when Monty had mixed himself up with a lot of bad people. We knew him from our weekly Thursday night potlucks at Vickie and Ruth's bungalow in Los Feliz. Kind and gentle, our Monty had renounced his former life and reinvented himself as a line cook at a halfway decent restaurant on Sunset, his former life marked by a permanent residue of motor grease under his nails.

It was tough to square.

A week after his funeral, holding court in Los Feliz from a ratty brown upholstered couch, his girlfriend Sharon was still trying to sort it out. It made no sense to her, what had happened to Monty. Having been with him for about eight months, she only knew Monty as a saint with stories.

Small-boned, graceful and athletic, Sharon was a couple years older than most of the group. Dark bangs cascaded over her forehead, matching her boldly outlined eyes. It was easy to picture her in a classroom, where she worked as an assistant teacher at Bright Lights Kindergarten in Sunset Park. She must have been the students' favorite, always luminous with no sharp edges.

She wondered if maybe Monty's death had something to do with last week's desecrated *Abbey Road* sign in West Hollywood. After all, Monty had worked just a few blocks away from it. So perhaps what happened to the billboard was no random act of vandalism. Instead, maybe it was something larger that Monty may have stumbled into at the restaurant, overheard an illicit plan that left him needing to be quieted.

We said, look, we loved Monty, but he'd had a past. It had to be acknowledged and accepted. And, yes, though he'd been in a better way over the last couple of years, there always are remnants. You have to be honest about this, we said. Who could really know?

Legs crossed, Sharon was leaned forward, pulling at the threads on the hems of her jeans. No, she said, shaking her head. She wasn't having it.

You could see her steaming. She bolted straight up, as if making to leave, but then sat down again, nearly collapsing back into place.

This was a tough time in our country and the world. We had seen a president shot in the street in broad daylight. We watched soldiers and the Vietnamese die on the nightly news. Police officers in Chicago had beat a young man holding an American flag. Black men targeted by cops and then jailed for defending themselves. For us, grasping at rationales had become a way of life. If, by chance, there were answers, you barely understood them.

Sharon blurted out, "Why are you all so hard on Monty? Why is your first response to blame him?"

She asked how we could just dismiss her idea about the billboard. Bad things don't just happen to good people for no reason.

"So why do you blame him?"

Bread and casseroles waited on the table in the dining room. Potato soup simmered on the stove. Scattered along the floor and against the walls, the five of us found ourselves politely smiling and urging ourselves toward compassion. The truth was that, since Monty died, we'd become Sharon's last connection to him.

Although it's not like we weren't heartbroken.

Sharon couldn't let go. Her musing about the missing head on Sunset took on sinister postulations: links to international intrigue, entertainment executives, and the Paul-is-dead conspiracy. She listened to "Strawberry Fields" backward and examined the cover of *Sgt. Pepper's Lonely Hearts Club Band* with a magnifying glass. She wrote letters to Apple Corps. She left messages with the secretaries at Capitol Records and even once trailed two executives when they left the building at lunch, trying to overhear their conversation. Her going theory was that there was a weak link in the conspiracy, someone intent on making sure that the public knew that Paul McCartney was dead. This was the person who had stolen the head on Sunset—a message to the believers—and who had, through inscrutable methods, somehow come to meet Monty. Perhaps this person had entrusted something to him or had given him a piece of information that he had no right to know.

We did try to reason with her, going for the most obvious point, which was that there was no reason to think that Paul was dead. For one thing, why would anyone have covered it up?

"Ask the British government," Sharon said. "And then the record company. They both know that the world couldn't handle the grief."

It was hard to argue with her when she was in grief herself. We left her alone, thinking that her theories were ultimately harmless and that they, too, would pass with the initial shock.

But then she went to the investigators who handled Monty's still-open case. They listened politely, seeing this for what it was; they were no strangers to such forms of speculation born from passion and grief. They never followed up on any of Sharon's suggestions, no matter how many times she called them. To Sharon, their reaction confirmed an obvious cover-up. Her paranoia grew; this was bigger than a billboard, bigger even than The Beatles. She started bringing up the Kennedys. Martin Luther King, Jr. Malcolm X. And how the authorities were aware of what she knew. Sharon came to believe that the only way to protect herself was to make sure that she told as many people as possible.

As her friends, we tried to err on the side of solicitude and understanding. As long as it stayed between all of us, we still believed that eventually, things would be okay.

But then she took her theories to her coworkers, lead teachers, and the parents. She said they had to be alerted. At drop-off, she would point to dark cars across the alley and warn the parents that they were being watched just for talking to her. She assured the children not to worry, that she would protect them. Complaints started drifting in. Recommendations for time off. For help.

We told her that maybe it wasn't such a bad idea to take some time away. That way, we reasoned on her level, there would be far less danger. For everyone.

"That won't do it," Sharon said. "I'd have to disappear entirely."

Vickie was alone when the authorities showed up at her house. A young woman social worker was framed by two burly cops who she let do the talking. This was all business. We felt horrible that Vickie had had to field this by herself. Anyone who'd experienced LAPD knew you could be cooked if they decided they were hungry for you. Based on the questions, it appeared that Bright Lights Kindergarten had initiated everything. The reason for this visit, one of the cops said, was to corroborate statements made regarding recent behaviors, particularly concerning statements Sharon had made about bringing a weapon to school. Whether that was for self-defense or for harming herself, we never learned for sure.

The school had documented everything. There was cause for alarm, the cop explained. Clipboard in hand, the social worker, stepping forward and nearly crossing into Vickie's duplex, called it "squaring the circle."

And what if Vickie had been able to stall for another day or so? Or what if the rest of us had been there?

The truth is that it wouldn't have mattered if we'd been there to back Vickie up. Those cops put her in a real position with their questions about Sharon. A true bind. The outcome of the official visit clearly was predetermined. This was no investigation. Its only purpose was to complete the record. What else was Vickie supposed to say? She'd later learn that Sharon had been involuntarily committed for a psychiatric evaluation the night before the LAPD showed up.

Sharon sent letters. Long letters that begged for assistance. She needed us to get to the newspapers. They had to know what was being done to her. She said the cover-up could no longer be her burden. That was the real reason she was there: to be shut up about what she discovered and to be hidden from public view. But we were useless. Not even trying to help.

The truth was, though we wouldn't have admitted it at the time, we were trying to forget all about her.

Several years later, Vickie went to visit Sharon at Metropolitan State Hospital, recently under scrutiny for the forced drugging of its patients. It was just the two of them in a common area, barely furnished other than some folded chairs against the wall and a long table near the back. Its cavernousness was striking. And while the room was hermitically quiet, you could hear voices from the warren of hallways as though they were right behind you.

The table was covered with a butcher block paper tablecloth with neatly arranged art supplies running down the center. In front of each chair was a brown grocery bag, the mismatched sacks representing various area markets. Sharon took a chair in front of an Alpha Beta bag, her name scrawled in permanent marker from someone else's hand. She gestured for Vickie to take the neighboring seat. The joints in her hands were pronounced, almost skeletal. Scanning the room, and, rolling her eyes for Vickie's benefit, Sharon said with an air of apology, "I mean the way some people live."

It wasn't as though she had any real expectations, yet it nearly floored Vickie to see Sharon not that much different than the last time she'd seen her in Los Feliz. If you discounted that Sharon was wearing slippers, a little underweight in a baggy gray sweatshirt, and that her pulled-back hair revealed a forehead that seemed more prominent and in a fixed state of concern, one might argue that she was strangely even more beautiful. But it was her walk that Vickie most noticed; flat-footed with her feet slightly angled, while her fingers, hands at her sides, opened and closed in descending fashion, over and over, as though they were the engine powering her.

We got all of this from Vickie after the fact. It had been eating at her, the feeling of complicity. We'd told her nothing was her fault, that she didn't report anything to the police that Sharon hadn't said, and that it was nothing more than dumb luck that she'd been the one who answered the door. It could have been any of us. She'd said we never understood what it meant, when the cops and the social workers had already made up their minds and all you could tell them was the truth.

Together, Vickie and Sharon sat at the long table in silence. Earlier, at the check-in desk, the attendant had said it was best not to bring up the past.

Echoes of voices swirled around them. If they couldn't speak of the past, what could they talk about?

Sharon stared off, massaging her forearm, pushing over and over on the tendon.

"What is in the bags?" Vickie finally asked.

A slim rectangle of light cut across the center of the table.

Without saying anything, Sharon stood up and reached into her Alpha Beta bag. Her eyes were watery. Movements slow and deliberate and without grace. She began pulling up little paper cut dolls from the sack, connected together, scissor people, some smooth and some chopped. One after the other. It was like a magician's trick. Every head had the same picture of Monty's face pasted on it, replicated from a photo snapped in Vickie and Ruth's living room, stained and streaked in a muddied blue ink from a ditto machine. Curling around the borders were random letters, and between them familiar symbols from religious and mystical texts.

Paper Montys.

She said, "I'm not supposed to talk about it."

Throughout the building, the chatter increased, now accompanied by a padded stampede of footsteps. It was nearing lunch.

Sharon said Vickie could take one. If she wanted.

Vickie didn't accept Sharon's offer. Later, she'd tell us she'd been afraid. That it was like breathing too close to a house of cards.

Sharon said she was hungry. It was lunchtime, and she needed to eat. She stepped away from the table, pushed her chair in, and arranged it with precision. Then she walked toward the entrance of the far corridor, leaving Vickie still seated at the table, her arms looped over her midsection, as though tied to the chair.

The ambient talk now sounded like it was coming from the walls. Vibrating. It could have been something phantasmagorical. It could have been an earthquake.

iii.

FOR YEARS after that afternoon, when Curtis Tibbs first approached him in the teacher's lot in the fall of 1969, Albie Thompson mulled over all the potential paths that his life might have taken if he had stayed later to correct papers in his homeroom. Or if he'd scheduled his meeting with the vice principal for that afternoon and not the previous, or if he'd decided to go for a beer with some of the other teachers. There were any number of possibilities. Instead, he'd made his way into the parking lot just as Curtis Tibbs, one year out of high school, happened to be at LAHS to pick up his freshman sister from school because their mother got called into work. It was only by chance that Albie had noticed Curtis's face, noticed that he was looking slack and pale as if he might faint. Normally he would have waved, intuitively knowing the things that were not his business. But on that September afternoon, with a pang of concern, he walked over to ask Curtis Tibbs if he was feeling okay. And the only way Curtis could respond was to hand his former US history teacher, Mr. Thompson, a balled-up piece of paper that, when unfolded, turned out to be a draft notice ordering Curtis to report for an Armed Services Physical Examination in two weeks at 8:58 a.m. And even then, things might have gone on as normal, with Albie expressing concern and trying to be reassuring, and then heading home. He would have spent the next two weeks focused on his lesson plans, teaching, and grading papers. He would have spent the next ten years going to his father's house at least once a week for dinner, maybe making the occasional drive up to Chavez Ra-

vine to see a Dodgers game, and, who knows, perhaps even shut-
tled future grandchildren for his father to watch. For a sliver of
time, any of that remained possible.

Until Curtis Tibbs, his eyes tearing as he looked up, relinquish-
ing any sense of pride he'd ever owned, said, "Mr. Thompson, I
could sure use one of those Underground Railroads about now."

What Curtis Tibbs could never have known is that once he'd
cried out for help, Albie was hooked into something that wouldn't
let go. Curtis Tibbs's situation had awakened the nagging shame
about never having done something meaningful. Albie had never
risked his own well-being for someone else. He talked about it
every day in the classroom. Baited and tried to inspire students to
take such a path. But he'd never truly put his convictions ahead
of his own comfort. The sacrifices always were best left to others;
after all, he had to be up by 6:30 on schooldays. Maybe everything would have turned out differently if that line of thinking
hadn't been fresh in his head when, on that September afternoon, he saw Curtis Tibbs in the parking lot. Maybe if that afternoon's class hadn't covered the abolitionist Levi Coffin, who
had sheltered somewhere around two-thousand runaway slaves
in his home as a stop on the Underground Railroad, despite never-ending threats to himself, his family, and friends, thus earning
a moniker begrudgingly bestowed upon him by his detractors but
conferred by history as *President of the Underground Railroad*.

"Okay," Albie said. "We'll figure something out."

Akin to the Underground Railroads he knew so well, Albie had
become networked with a SUPA contact in the States. He never
knew who he was speaking with, only that he initially called a
phone booth with a 510 area code; from that point on, he was
phoned by the SUPA contact at prearranged times. Those calls
produced the plan that would ferry Curtis to Canada.

On a Sunday morning, while Curtis Tibbs and his family were
still in church, it was decided that Curtis would leave on Monday
night, three days before his scheduled physical. He'd layover in
Portland, Oregon, with someone who would be revealed to him

upon arrival and sleep in that person's basement for two nights. Then a new secret driver would take him the rest of the way into British Columbia, where members of the Vancouver Committee to Aid American War Objectors would further assist him in a basic resettlement plan. The plan was loose. There was mystery in the seams. But there was no reason to believe there would be any hitches or danger, as long as Curtis was long gone before his appointment with the Armed Services.

It's never been clear whether Curtis Tibbs was discovered on his way to Canada or whether he had turned back on his own. The facts, as Albie knew them, were that they'd made it up I-5 as far north as Redding. In any case, something happened between Curtis using the telephone at a truck stop and then coming back to the VW to say he needed to take a leak before they hit the road. The next place Curtis Tibbs was located was at a diner counter in a truck stop outside of Fresno, California, where he sat for four hours without moving, waiting while his parents trudged up the Grapevine and through the Central Valley to retrieve their shaking son.

Between the time the Tibbs family was en route back from Fresno to Los Angeles, Albie had been put on notice by an emergency call from his SUPA contact that Tibbs had left, and that the plan was compromised. They said because the only name that Curtis Tibbs could offer the FBI was that of Mr. Alban Thompson, Albie ought to best disappear, lest the whole network go down. Vanish. Right away. Before it was too late. They were sending someone now. Just lay low until you get the next set of directions. Albie left the papers he was grading on the table. He packed his bag. Drained his bank account. And in under two hours, he was out his back door and climbing into a white van.

Albie didn't feel as though he had to slink out of town; he'd already vanished. They stopped at the Gulf on Wilshire for gas, just before getting on the freeway, and Albie got out of the back, took a brazen first step as a fugitive inside the minimart, and bought two packs of M&M's, so adept at ghosting through the aisles that even the cashier didn't notice him.

As it turned out, the very next morning, Curtis Tibbs, escorted by his old man, reported a day early for his physical, with no questions asked. After dropping his son off, Tibbs' father, a veteran, had gone straight to the FBI. By then, Albie was well past Redding and not far from Portland, where he'd take the bed Curtis Tibbs was supposed to be sleeping in. Three weeks later, Albie was renamed Percy Roth in Canmore, Alberta. And four months later, Curtis Tibbs was dead on a battlefield in the Mekong Delta.

iv.

IT'S TRUE the waiter had told us they were out of romaine, but we hadn't expected the salad to be made of basil.

The woman who would become my wife said, "What the hell?" and though I didn't want to make a production, I did have to admit it was no way to eat a salad, even if they had sprinkled the top with some carrots, croutons, and radishes.

This was one of those eateries where you sit at the counter, and you can see the cooks back in the kitchen. The cook could see we were boiling. The woman who would become my wife, she was especially hungry. She'd been back and forth across the valley all day for work, and she'd had no time to eat anything but a stale muffin. She wanted something fresh. That was her only request. I didn't say the obvious. The timing was all wrong.

"Flag him down," she said, referring to the waiter. But he knew what was what. He was keeping to the other side of the floor.

It was a funny time at the restaurant, right on the cusp—after the dinner hour, but just before the nightclub people would start to roll in. A San Francisco band was playing up the street at the Whiskey. Looking out the window, you could spot their fans coming up the block.

She pushed the so-called salad away, the plate dangerously close to the edge of the counter. For a moment, I thought it would fall off. She was making a point. The cook was watching. You could only see his eyes, peering over the few tickets that hung down over his line. Something about him was familiar. It was impossible to tell if he was trying to make eye contact or if he was trying to avoid us.

She said we should just go. That this was bullshit. Outside, the sidewalks were filling with more and more people making their way to the clubs. Even our dumb little eatery was beginning to fill up.

I said, "We'll never get into any place else at this point."

I suggested we try to order her something else.

"In this ghost town?"

He was like an angel, that chef. He appeared behind the counter, delivering a plate of freshly sautéed vegetables, mostly greens, layered over rice. It wasn't quite the fresh that she'd been after, but it was generous and kind, and it was close enough. He apologized to the woman who would become my wife, saying the kid had told him it was okay.

"But once you got the plate, I could tell by your face that he was an idiot."

The chef pulled a waste bin out from under the counter, and, in a symbolic gesture meant as an act of confederacy, he tilted the basil salad into the bin.

She thanked him, although it wasn't clear if it was for the vegetable dish or for getting rid of that ridiculous salad. Probably both.

The chef braced both hands on the counter, leaning his weight into it. I could feel his breath. See the two whiskers he'd missed shaving, right at the line of his lower lip. He knotted his eyes, as if bringing me into focus. He was slick and put together, although the preening confidence appeared fragile.

"Do we know each other?" he asked me.

I said he looked familiar. But I couldn't place it.

"Anything to do with go-kart racing by any chance?"

The woman who would become my wife laughed and brought her napkin off her lap to her mouth, in case she spit out some broccoli.

He shrugged. "No, I'm serious." He was used to it, the reaction. "I'm sorry," she said.

"It was another life," he said. "A former line of work is all."

For a week, it picked at me how I knew him. I could picture having once spoken with him, though I couldn't remember the context of the conversation, just that it had happened. I knew that it took place when I was younger, before I had met the woman who would become my wife. Those were the years when all I craved was connection, when you have the sense that any person that you might meet could be the one to change your life.

In the middle of the week, I went back to the diner. I wanted to figure it out. The same waiter was there. He didn't recognize me. You could tell this wasn't a job he cared about. This kid was just killing time until the next thing.

I had to go up to the counter and stand in front of the cash register to get his attention. I fingered the toothpick jar while trying to glimpse into the kitchen.

"Table for one?" he asked.

I said I was looking for the cook who worked in the evenings. He was here about a week ago.

"You mean Monty?"

The name rang a bell, but I couldn't be sure.

"Kind of tall," I said. "Thin."

"Yeah." The kid's face got funny. He cleared his throat once or twice. Dug his hands into the front of his apron. He apologized, saying he hadn't had to say it yet. At least not to a stranger. No matter what you thought of this waiter, you could see he was struggling. That it was hard. I felt for this kid, this sweet idiot kid, who was about to give me horrible news.

I found myself backing up. It was reflexive. And then I stepped forward again and took a seat at the counter. I asked him for a glass of water. I was pretty sure I was going to pass out.

The kid filled up a pitcher, pouring a glass for me and then one for himself. He said he didn't know what happened, only that it happened, and it seemed like it was really rough. He said

Monty was a nice guy, but it seemed like he was mixed up in some bad things. And then he asked how I knew him.

"That's the thing . . ."

The kid sipped his water. I never finished the thought, and he didn't care. He wasn't really that interested. He had his own thoughts and his own worries. He said there seemed to be a curse on this block. Along the whole strip.

"There's been nothing but a spate of bad luck. Bad news piled on top of bad news. Ever since that head got taken."

That night, at the apartment of the woman who would become my wife, I told her about Monty, about how I didn't know how I knew him but that I felt hit as though I did. And then I told her what the kid had said about the bad luck and the curse ever since that business with the sign, and we both agreed that it was possible and that we hoped that they found that Paul McCartney head soon. We didn't need any more bad news in this world.

Head in the Hills

i.

JUST BEFORE midnight, Cassie asked Michael if maybe they weren't getting the most out of life. Maybe they kept trying to shove the wrong pieces into the puzzle.

At eighteen-and-a-half, nowhere to go, and the draft lottery breathing down his neck, it was tough for Michael to imagine how to get anything in this life past basic maintenance.

It was on *Satan* Monica Boulevard near Barney's Beanery, which they had been loitering outside of since 10:30, hoping to spot a rock star who might want to party with them and share his stash. The closest they'd gotten was a Byrd who they couldn't quite place and who willfully ignored them on his way in.

"Come to think of it," she mused as they gave up and walked away, "maybe it's *right pieces, wrong puzzle.*"

A light breeze blew over them, cool and smelling of ocean salt and exhaust.

Ducking into a bus shelter, Cassie pulled a pipe out from the inside pocket of her jean jacket and steadied it while Michael scraped its sides with a ballpoint pen, trying to dislodge the last of the crusted hash.

"The problem with puzzles," he said, digging at the pipe's walls, "is that you get trapped into remaking someone else's story, as perfect and beautiful as it seems."

"At least it's something beautiful."

"Even the most beautiful of butterflies only lives for a matter of days."

Cassie bent forward and pushed his headband up for him. "Beauty and grace. I'll take it every time."

She and Michael had met in a conceptual art class during a mutually short stint in junior college. They'd necked like mad during a night of partying until some warning sign flashed red in both their brains to stop them from going to bed and ruining everything. Since then, they'd become fully devoted.

Michael lit the pipe, drawing in smoke and pulling it down. For a moment, it felt like the resin holding all the disparate parts of his being together.

She asked if he'd noticed the near euphoria in people trying to see and experience that billboard head.

"In a way," she said, "I'm so moved by how such joy can come out of a violent act."

As he tilted his head up and slowly exhaled, Michael actually could see himself gliding along the trail of smoke.

"You know, you're a dead ringer," Cassie said, shaking her head. "I've never even noticed this until now. If you took off that headband and combed your bangs down, you'd look like Paul. A real dead ringer."

"Maybe the cartoon version from those Saturday morning shows."

"Close enough." She grabbed the pipe, sucked off the last hit, and then, linking her arm with Michael's, took a giant goose step out of the bus shelter.

Michael closed his eyes and let her march him into the warm darkness.

Walking up the block, she talked and talked about a kind of theater that was needed to capture the essence of what was happening with that billboard on Sunset. One with no script, in which the audience became the performers, and in turn, the performers became in total existence with the world. A common euphoria. One in which everyone would become the puzzle and its pieces.

But as she talked, her words narrowed into a single idea that began to scare him. It needed to happen tomorrow, she said, while interest in the head was still at its peak. For Michael, the world was just the kind of thing he tried to avoid, its threats and assignations. But he couldn't bring himself to do anything other than agree to meet her on Sunset in the morning because despite being so strong in stature, with her confidence and her belief in *the positive*, underneath it all, Cassie was so fragile. It was one of the great mysteries to Michael, if he thought about it, how someone could simultaneously be lost *and* found.

Moving up the Strip the next morning, Cassie stepped forward and tapped the arms of passers-by, chanting *Rejoice the head of Paul McCartney*. A step behind her, Michael, costumed in a black cloak, with his bangs combed down and eyeliner to make his eyes look a little bigger, simulated the Paul McCartney head floating by. He kept tugging at the ties around his neck that hitched the robe to his body. It felt like they were choking him.

This was the realization of Cassie's vision, her *happening* on Sunset Boulevard. A street show of humanity and harmony in homage to the missing billboard head.

On the way to meet her, Michael had scored a little something from some freaks hanging out near the Whiskey, just enough to calm his nerves for the pending public display. Now looking up, he swore he saw his own head disembodied and sailing out over the hills. To ground himself, he began cooing "Blackbird," but it wasn't him singing. He knew his own shitty voice. It was McCartney's, pure and liquid, a voice more familiar than the one that came out of his mouth.

Amid all the tourists and the brunchers, freaks and hangers-on, gazers and peepers, all of them enthralled by the circus of the desecrated *Abbey Road* billboard, Michael let her lead him up Sunset, playing the part of a floating head that, with each step, he feared was becoming a reality.

Near the Fred C. Dobbs Coffeehouse, Michael first noticed the boy. Backed against the storefront, as if to keep clear of the sidewalk, he held his mother's hand, craning his neck as Michael and Cassie passed. Dressed in striped blue pants, brown

boots, and a short-sleeve maroon pullover, the boy homed right
in on Michael's eyes, the dark eyeliner starting to run down in
the corners.

Michael could tell the boy was on to him. That he saw Michael being overtaken. He wanted to say *stop staring*. *Don't look at
me again. Ever*. But all he heard was Paul McCartney's voice coming out of him, still singing "Blackbird."

The boy just stared. He must have heard it too.

When Michael turned around to continue Cassie's *rejoicing* up
the block, he no longer saw the Strip. He no longer saw anything
before him. Instead, he was watching himself through the boy's
eyes, an attestant who could later testify to seeing the McCartney
head floating up Sunset. An eyewitness who'd confirm there was
nothing for Michael to do except to start running, jetting away
from Cassie, who, unawares, kept dancing around in abbreviated
loops, one hand floating above her head and sprinkling imaginary pixie dust.

Through the boy's eyes, Michael could see his own helplessness, grasping at the knot that secured the cloak, pulling on it
to free his body from the head, tugging, his fingers prying and
twisting, and how it wouldn't come off, the tie cord only digging
into his neck, scraping and scratching and burning and choking.

McCartney's voice still boomed, vibrating his bones from the
inside out.

Michael ran, and he ran, until, just before the actual billboard,
he disappeared off the Strip and up toward the hills. He pushed
against the dry Santa Anas that came gusting in, desperate to be
lost to the world forever, his headband dangling out of his back
pocket like a flag of surrender, begging the boy to stop looking,
already terrified that what he and the boy were seeing would become an imprinted memory, one that would stay with both of
them when they'd face worse things in the future, things you'd
want to forget.

ii.

ON AN empty road in the Hollywood Hills, a man and a woman appear in the beam of a pair of headlights. It's the dead of night—far from the evening but nowhere near morning. The woman sits on a dirt mound, her knees drawn into her chest, arms looped around them, head down and shaking. Dead grass stalks, long and brown, blow away from her with each breath of wind. The neck hole of her T-shirt is torn, grabbed and stretched, hanging limply. The man, standing spotlighted in the beam, waves his hands, trying to draw attention. Four distinct lines of blood trail along his forehead. His face looks distorted and exaggerated—a thin, nearly translucent smear of red along his philtrum blooms in a watercolor mustache. His right eye has swollen into an exaggerated squint. They both wear jeans. Both lanky. And at first glance, both could be seen as the graduate students they are. He keeps flagging his hands in the headlights—palms open, arms rhythmically crossing over each other—until the car slows down and pulls over. The night is so quiet that the tires rolling along the gravel on the side of the road sound like thunder.

They are at least three-quarters of a mile from the closed gas station where they'd squeezed into the phone booth together, the booth lit up, and the door folded closed. Still frightened despite the reprieve, they'd called for help, surrounded by graffiti scratched and penknifed into the glass, mostly unintelligible other than the multiple *fuck*s and *suck*s and *pussie*s. It would be a half-hour drive to get them, at least, at this time of night. They said they'd be walking east along the middle-of-nowhere Hollywood Hills roadside. Maybe it would have made more sense to keep visible, be protected by the yellow night lights of the gas station and the vanilla glow of the phone booth, but, driven purely by instinct, there was something almost compulsive about finding a place to hide in the dark.

In the back of the car is a boy, a nine-year-old boy, pulled out of his bed by his mother, a single mother. After getting the phone call, awoken from a deep sleep, and accepting the collect charges of a local call, she'd had to decide if she should leave her son in bed sleeping while she motored off out of Santa Monica and into the Hollywood Hills to rescue her friends. Logically, she knew she'd be back before he awoke, but then again, it seemed like something really was wrong, and who knew what that might entail. Cops? Hospitals? Plus, who could say what time she'd actually get home? It was too late to call anyone. Her boyfriend, the actor, also a friend to the stranded couple, was staying the night at his father's, a movie legend, following a late-night strategy session for how to pitch his recently secured movie rights to a book everyone seemed to love. There was no way she could call so late. Out of options, she lifted the boy from his bed, still wrapped in his wool blanket. She carried him outside, hugging him while going down the two cement steps and then along the walk, before threading him through the open door and laying him across the backseat of her Porsche 356. There was no right answer.

The man helps the woman rise up from the mound. They hug the driver. They say they are sorry. Dazed, they all stand there, the hills rugged and quiet, a world away from the sparkling agate lights of the city below them.

The driver, the boy's mom, asks what happened. She can see the trauma. She is the witness to it.

"It was unbelievable," the man begins. His voice quivers. "We were . . ." Then he spots the boy laid out in the back of the car. "Oh, Christ." He interrupts himself.

His hands dig into his back pockets while he nods his head. He says he's made a mess and that he didn't mean to make such a production when he called. He never meant for the boy to be involved. It never even occurred to him.

Together, the three of them now turned Samaritans on behalf of the boy, lift him, blanket-clad, into the front seat. The man raises his chin up, head tilted back, cautious not to drip blood on the child or stain his blanket.

The man and the woman climb into the back, broken, all adrenaline drained, muscles and limbs jellied. From the front seat can be heard the occasional sniffle and sob coming from behind. Otherwise, it is quiet in the car, quieter than even the hillside, and the rumbling engine doesn't sound mechanical, it sounds like the core of the earth.

The boy stares out the front window. Into a pitch-black dark that occasionally sparks with streaks of distant city lights blazing across the windshield. He's not sure if he's sleeping. Not sure why Tom and Julieta are in the backseat. Not sure why any of this is happening. Only that it's so familiar, as if he's seen it all before.

The early morning light turns the vinyl shade orange. It's drawn down as far as it can go, bulging out over the sill. In its center is a vague shadow, outlining the semi-modern apartment building across the street, where the legendary L.A. Lakers guard Jerry West is reputed to live. A housefly keeps banging at its bottom, over and over again. Buzzing and trying to get through the glass.

Tom is stretched across the couch, knees bent and angled, the spare comforter pulled up under his chin. The pocket beneath his right eye is outlined like a perfect half-moon, swollen and black. He rolls over, his pillow slipping to the floor. Pulling the comforter up further, he exposes his green-socked feet and the hem of his blue jeans.

He opens his eye, the good one, the working one, while the injured one remains resolutely shut. Wearing blue pajamas dotted with airplanes, the boy is looking right at him. Tom feels studied. As though he's some kind of character being written on the spot. He tells the boy *good morning* in something that is less a voice and more of a clever manipulation, sounds and utterances dragging along the crag of his throat that replicate language.

The boy keeps his distance. He puts a finger to his lips. He says, "We need to be *more quiet*. Everyone else still is sleeping."

It is just the two of them, the boy and Tom. The boy's mom has not risen—it being Saturday, and it being the morning after a late night. Julieta shares the bed with her. Tom had insisted that he would not put his host and rescuer on the couch.

Each time Tom moves his face, the previous night's severity is revealed. No longer just the remnants of scratches and claw marks, it looks like a true injury. His hand creeps out from under the comforter. It's still dirty and messy, dried brown muck and nearly open scabs. He curls himself into the back of the couch and pats the middle cushion.

"Sit down," he whispers, doing everything he can not to sound sinister, which is not so easy.

The boy tiptoes over, the airplanes on his pajamas each like little engines, flying him toward Tom, as though this were not his living room, but a Pacific island that's remote and unfamiliar. The boy takes a seat, and the cushion dips a little.

Tom groans, more like he's sustaining an injury, but then he breathes out deeply and tries to smile. Probably the boy wants to know what this is all about, how he ended up here, but it's complicated, and nothing Tom would ever share with him. But he does have something to give the boy, a bright side, a confirmation concerning a magical occurrence that the boy had witnessed a week ago on Sunset. Only Tom, who cares equally as much about The Beatles, had taken an interest in the boy's reporting. Everyone else had dismissed it as either silly, imaginative, or an illusion caused by the spectacle of the Strip. But Tom had asked questions. He was willing to believe.

Jackknifing, Tom lifts himself up and gets a little closer to the boy. Inches from the boy's ear, Tom says that he saw it.

The boy shrugs.

Again, Tom says he saw it. He can't say where exactly, or at what point in the night, because it was a crazy night, and it all blends together with the blank spots, but somewhere in there, he tells the boy, he saw it. Hiding behind a bush.

Finally, the boy asks him to say what he saw, sensing what's coming.

Tom looks at him like it's obvious. As though they are picking up in the middle of a conversation they've been having all week. He says he saw the head. He says he saw Paul McCartney's head.

Later in the morning, his mom's boyfriend, the actor, sits on the edge of the chair, leaning forward and rubbing his hands together. He is handsome, a carefully crafted face that bears many of the hallmarks of his legendary father—strong jawline, pronounced but sculpted nose, lancing blue eyes, permanently windswept hair—and yet there is something softer about his features, a little more gentle than his father's, perhaps something he got from his mother. But today, his eyes are narrowed, and when he pauses to think, they drift upward to the left as though searching for the missing words to fill out his thoughts. He keeps asking how it happened. Why it happened. What exactly did happen.

At the end of the couch, the folded comforter is topped by two pillows, leaning and sinking with each movement. Squished into the middle of the sofa, Julieta scoots in uncomfortably toward Tom. It is not affection. Nor is it comfort. It is protection, as though she is curling herself into a ball, her head and her vital organs tucked under and sheltered from harm.

The boy sprawls out on his bedroom floor, the door propped open wide enough that he hears the conversation. He hears his mother flitting back and forth from the kitchen, making coffee, preparing breakfast, asking questions from another room, and never staying in one place too long. There is a world in front of the boy, a village dominated by toy cars, mostly Dinkys that his grandmother bought for him on an overseas trip, a collection that she continues to enhance with occasional additions from her travels. And they motor in and around each other, adventures and emergencies, heists and occasions, the black Rolls Royce Phantom, the station wagon Rescuer Ambulance, the Mustang Fastback, the Pontiac Parisienne, the double-decker bus, the Ford Lincoln Continental, a VW Bug and a Karmann Ghia, Batmobile and Yellow Submarine (the last two actually made by Corgi, but they fit in), and then, off to the side and special, the Porsche 356, deep deep red, a near replica of the ones his mother and the actor drive, minus the color. Moving the cars back and forth. Maintaining their storyline. That takes enough attention to negotiate.

The actor presses. "I still don't understand," he says. "I don't get how it turned into an event in the middle of the night. Why didn't you call the police?"

Julieta is diminutive in stature, slender and petite in all ways—tiny shoulders, tiny nose and ears, hands delicate as a doll's—and yet her voice can carry and boom in a variety of pitches and textures, one that she uses for wages when she dubs and translates the voices for *Looney Tunes* characters for broadcast in Spain and Mexico, going straight to her graduate school tuition at UCLA for Latin American Literature. But she can't seem to raise the slightest trace of her voice today. Mute and without language.

Tom speaks slowly. "We couldn't call the cops."

The actor bends closer to them. His arms extend. Exasperated. He asks why not. "Look at the both of you. And they stole your car, too?"

Tom explains it was a bad situation. Poor judgment. They were following bad advice, he says. A bad lead.

Julieta, still pushed in tight to Tom, mutters, "Creeps."

They both stop talking and listen to her.

"Fucking creeps." And then, as though it is something physiological, she sinks back within herself.

The actor looks conflicted. He doesn't trust the cops any more than anyone else. He's seen what they did to the kids protesting on Sunset. How they handled the riots in Watts. He's watched them batter anti-war protestors at UCLA and other campuses, witnessed in person and on TV. And yet, look at his friends when left on their own, beaten and battered.

"We were making a buy, okay?" Tom says. "A deal. But it was shit, it was a shit deal. A shit circumstance, and so there is no way we could tell the cops because we blew it, because one of the dealers *was* a cop. Okay, we blew it. Really screwed up."

Julieta asks if they can talk about it later. She says it is too much right now, and for the moment, she doesn't want to relive it. In fact, she *never* wants to relive it.

She says, "Let's all agree to pretend that nothing ever happened." In the voice she uses for dubbing Porky Pig's outro at the end of every *Looney Tunes* cartoon, Julieta declares ¡*Eso es todo, amigos!*

Then she stands up, turns an imaginary lock over her heart, and, bringing her hand up to her mouth, she swallows the imaginary key. The pillows and the comforter tumble onto the floor. For a moment, she is trapped, caught between Tom's gangly legs and the pile of bedding. She turns in each direction, unsure of which way to go. She looks like she could cry. Stepping left, Julieta heads for the kitchen, directed purely by momentum.

Tom leans in closer to the actor. His forehead scrunches, opening the corner of one of the wounds, where a trickle of fresh blood pools but doesn't fall. He confesses there was another reason for not calling the cops, beyond the threats and intimidation. It is one of fraternity, one of sanguinity, one of affinity and fellowship. He says he didn't want to involve the actor. He didn't want to risk his name being dragged into this, a risk to his acting career and to the movie rights he's after. And, in a more distant way, to the actor's father, not because he cared so much about the legend, but only because he knew the legend never would forgive his son if his reputation got pulled into a dope dealing police scandal.

From the kitchen come the sounds of ceramic plates chiming as they're lifted out of the cupboard, the percussion of forks and knives scooped from the drawer, coffee cups and Shell giveaway juice glasses, and the vacuum of the refrigerator door opening and closing.

Meanwhile, in the back bedroom, the boy remains on the floor, driving his toy metal cars in circles, up roads, up the blankets, and up the side of the bed, tooling around through the Hollywood Hills, slowly and carefully. Someone is in need of rescue.

By early evening, after going in for a midday nap, Tom and Julieta have not come out of his mom's bedroom. A streak of light glows under the door. It feels barricaded.

The actor, having sat all day at the dining room table working on the proposal, closes the book and sets down his pen. He announces to the boy's mom that he gives up.

"I can barely focus with all of this going on." He looks back to the bedroom door. "It's just weird, is all. Too weird." He says, despite everything, all he can do is judge.

In his room, the boy still pushes his cars around, searching through the hills and canyons of his blankets. He's thinking about how much he really likes the actor. How safe he feels with him there. The boy thinks the actor is always trying to do the right thing, calm and cool at all times, the way you imagine people are supposed to be.

The boy's mom confesses that earlier in the kitchen, Julieta declared that for now, she wanted to be like the boy, a child protected in his mother's home. She said she didn't want to leave. Not for a while. At least not for the foreseeable future.

"She doesn't even want the curtains or blinds opened. And I don't want to sound like . . . But I can't have them living here like that. Not indefinitely. I don't know what to do."

Driving the black Rolls Royce Phantom through the crevices and canyons of his blankets, the boy pushes it up and over a wrinkled tuft, stopping it beside the Mustang Fastback. Speaking on behalf of the Rolls Royce driver, he asks, *Did you find the Paul McCartney head yet?* The Mustang driver answers, *I've been searching all morning, but I just can't locate it. High and low. All around. Don't know what to do.* About to direct them *over there*, the boy pauses the cars in place. Suddenly he no longer sees them from above, but instead, he's spying on them from ground level, behind the sagebrush, suspicious, lost for words, uncertain if being rescued is the same as being found.

iii.

SHE SAYS that if she were to write a memoir, she's not sure when she would use *Cassie* and when she would use *Cassandra* for the narrator, having been known as the latter for the past forty years, with the former being her sixties name. She's in the Community Center, where out the window the redwoods bend just enough

that she can see the rocky cove. At the weekly midday tea, a social hour to break things up, she manages to make her seat at the
round table seem as though she's sitting at the head. The memoir
topic is a version of a conversation people regularly engage her
in. Fascinated by her verbal perambulations about her past, a
free-spirited witness to a glamourous world, they always kick her
off with questions like who she'd imagine would play her in the
movie about her life. To this particular audience of five, four of
them familiar and one not, she goes on to remark that Cassie and
Cassandra are two different people. If she were ever to write a
memoir, she knows that it would be impossible to connect Cassie
to who she became. That's why she doesn't know which name
she'd use, she explains. They're not interchangeable.

There's the hippy beatnik arthouse girl who nearly lost her way,
freewheeling and reckless, who later went back to school (UCLA,
summa cum laude), then law school (UCLA, Order of the Coif,
never touching the law again after being handed her diploma).
And then there's the one who returned to art after a decade in
Europe (Oslo) by opening a gallery in Southern California (Santa
Monica) that did well enough among a select group of celebrity
buyers to put her in *People* magazine and to fund her retirement at
her present community among the redwoods up the coast. And
then there are the three husbands that made sense in their time,
but with whom she now couldn't even imagine carrying on a complete conversation over dinner, if she even knew where any of her
former husbands were, and what order they'd come in.

That last line always wins a laugh, even for those who know
it's coming. The new man at the table, called Gary, says she
should forget a memoir. The degree to which he is smitten with
her is obvious to all. Every new resident has felt it at one time or
another. Gary declares that instead of a book, they should make
a TV series about her.

"Right," she says. "We'll call it: *A Storied Life Without a Story.*"

Here's what she's learned: People prefer the glamour. They prefer
Cassandra. They want the anecdotes about the movie stars who

came to her gallery, the behind-the-scenes secrets they shared, and the misdeeds she witnessed. They are curious about her time in Norway, always rationed out somewhat mysteriously. Zigzagging in and out of parties and events that suggest a rank of nobility, the details are rarely revealed, leading many to think that for one of her marriages, she had been part of the royal family. Others envisioned her having been a CIA agent, a ludicrous ascription for someone who came of age as a Southern California flower child. But, adopting the gold standard of that clandestine spy industry, she has learned neither to confirm nor deny. She likes the mystery. She prefers people imagining her over actually knowing her.

Gary requests something specific. He asks for something of the Cassie vein. "Give us a taste of her," he asks. "A little nibble."

There is one story, an origin story that she tells rarely, only when she's in the company of new people, mainly men like Gary and others his age. As she tells it, she'll scan their faces, looking for traces of recognition, hoping one of them can provide her with the eventual ending.

It takes place on a December day in 1969, a day that started off cloudy and could have brought the first and only rain of the month, a misfortune of timing to spoil her plan. But as with all the days that month, the sun broke through, and Cassie took it as a sign, a cosmic hand of encouragement. She gives background about the billboard, the McCartney head, Cassie's growing dissatisfaction with her place in the world, and, just for a touch of verisimilitude, she includes Cassie's love of smoking hash. It's when she peppers Michael into the tale that Cassandra first looks up to catch a reaction.

Maybe Gary was there? Maybe he knows Michael? And as she talks about costuming her companion as a "Paul McCartney Head" for a happening on the Strip, she continues to glance at Gary, trying to determine if this rings a bell. But Gary, like the others, is leaned forward, arms on the table. He is a rapt audience member, nothing more.

She talks about dancing up the Strip. Michael's costume. She accounts for the exact amount of money they raised in the hat (three dollars and twenty-six cents) that Michael insisted would be used to score more hash. She tells it like recalling scenes from a movie. She remembers becoming so lost in the experience. Absorbed by the purity of beauty. The one and only point in her life that she totally was in herself and out of herself at the same time, both as a member of the human race and as part of Gaia herself. When Cassie looked up, though, Michael wasn't there. She spun around, trying to see if she could spot him. But it was all without urgency. This was a bubble of joy. People were laughing along and dancing, gathering around her and becoming her and her becoming them, and it was beautiful and more than she might have imagined. She figured Michael must have gotten lost in the experience. She'd been certain she heard his voice. It was only after they reached the base of the billboard that Cassie realized he was gone. Nowhere to be seen. She called his name. Walked further up, and then turned around the other way. Calling and calling. Out of all those people on the sidewalk, the only person she remembers is a small boy being led away by his mom. But Michael had vanished. Only later would she realize it was forever.

For a short time, she had thought he had been part of her imagination, a companion conjured in her conceptual art class, something to soothe her own fear of being adrift. But when friends had started asking after him, and she realized she had no answer, Cassie had taken herself back to the Strip. Starting in front of Gazzarri's, near the corner of Doheny, she had marched up toward the billboard, reconstructing each moment. Looking up at the craggy hills, and scanning the huddled sidewalks that showed no trace of Michael, Cassie was forced to concede that she had been so self-absorbed during her happening that she had forgotten about him, something that to this day has killed any sense of the pure pleasure she felt that afternoon, and instead stiffened her into someone who became inclined to control every situation, staving off anything or anyone that threatens her vigilance.

Gary asks what she'd call that chapter in her memoir.

"That chapter?" Cassandra considers. She says she'd title it:
"Regret."

Walking back to her condo, Cassandra takes the long way. It's the
path that winds along the edge of the grounds, on the tall cliff
that overlooks the rocky cove. A waist-high wooden fence meant
for safety also designates it as a frontier, meant to signal to beach-
combers that this area is not for the public. But sometimes, she
wonders if it is meant as a corral, designed to keep its residents
from impulsively acting on their worst impulses.

Below, she can hear the waves breaking against the rocks, impossible to see through the fog that has begun to roll in. Soon,
it will climb off the water's surface, rising and engulfing their
grounds, leaving only the tops of the redwoods poking through
the spray of yellow lights coming through apartment windows.
So predictable this time of year, this time of day.

Behind her, she hears footsteps, and they sound hurried, has-
tening. When they appear to come closer, she also notices panting,
like a steam engine on its last load of coal, trying to push up the
mountain.

"Excuse me."

She recognizes Gary's voice.

"Pardon me, Cassandra."

This is the moment she wishes for, when a stranger, after hearing her story, will tell her he knows something about Michael, or,
even better, is Michael himself. But she knows the wish will be
unfulfilled. It's never even been close. She slows down, allowing
him to catch up to her. He moves slower than expected, stiff-
hipped, legs swinging side to side, nearly unable to keep ahead
of the drifting fog.

He says, "I don't mean to disturb you."

"Shh," she says, drawing her finger to her lips. She nods to the
cove. "Have you ever heard anything quite that lovely?"

As the fog starts to drift upward, she lifts her chin, letting the
moisture coat her face. She pats down her hair as she turns to
face him. "You wanted to tell me something?"

"I only wanted to say that I didn't mean to say you shouldn't write a memoir."

Cassandra smiles. "It's all just talk. . . . Talk, talk, talk." She gazes down at the disappearing cove. "My god, have you ever seen something so beautiful?"

iv.

HE SAYS . . .

And you say . . .

And he says, "You want to know about irony, well, here's irony: It's fifty years later, and I'm still hustling out on the streets to get money for drugs, only this time the drugs are legal and meant to keep my head straight. Not to convince people on Sunset Boulevard that my head is Paul McCartney's."

He pauses, eyeing you, waiting to see if you'll flinch. It's hard to tell if he wants you to see him as being funny or shocking or just plain crazy. The best thing to do, per the training manual, is to nod. Acknowledge. Show that he's being heard. Sometimes that's not so easy.

"Never mind," he says. "I don't know why I bother. For a moment, I forgot this was a place of business. That we're all part of your bottom line. Your profits."

"Michael," you say, your voice steady. You pause, allowing the piped-in music to reach him. It's meant to soothe. A psychologist designed the space. He anticipated most everything. You can't tell Michael there is some truth to what he says. While his veteran's benefits have been in limbo for the better part of a year due to a snafu that a recent piece of legislation didn't remediate, it is true, in the abstract, that the government continues to earn interest on those unallocated funds. And while "profit" might not be the most precise word, for the sake of this conversation and Michael's predicament, it is good enough. You can't tell him any of that, though. What you can say, is:

"We're here to help."

He says *we* can help by getting his benefits paid to him. He served his country. Now it ought to serve him, not tie him up in bureaucratic loopholes that force him to come up with crazy ways to get his meds.

You ask if that explains the arrest on the subway.

"Citation," he corrects. "I wasn't arrested."

"Fair enough," you say. His folder is stuffed, from commendations to medical records to details of benefits. "But a criminal record will only complicate things."

He asks what you're going to do about it.

"About it?"

"Getting my benefits back. I need my meds. I need a place to live. Why are you doing this to me?"

You tell him it's not *you*.

"You are the bureaucracy." He looks like he could explode, not in an angry way, but in an incredulous way. There is a difference.

He says . . .

And you say . . .

He says . . .

And you say . . .

He says . . .

And you say . . .

He says . . .

And you say . . .

Michael stands up. He says he imagines you've met long enough for you to mark him present and accounted for this month.

"It is important to document that you're coming to your regularly scheduled appointments."

"I want to go now. . . . I've got to get to 30th Street to scare up a bed for tonight." He stops and turns around. You can smell the street on him. With his hands braced on the back of his chair, Michael leans forward. His shoulders hunch up to his ears. He says, "If it's okay, I have one more question."

You say, "I'll try to help."

He says, "Where were you in 1969? Or, maybe I should ask, how old were you in 1969?"

According to the training manual, any personal information of the Claims Specialist should not be shared with the claimant. It even goes so far as to warn that this can be a strategy in which the claimant tries to subvert the process in an effort to manipulate the specialist into breaking with procedure. The manual notes that many of the clients are skilled in the art of misdirection and persuasion in order to deceive. Trying to create a sympathetic relationship is one of the most common tactics.

He says, "Are you doing the math in your head or something?"

"Michael," you say, remembering to keep a steady voice so he will not see any of your actions as a threat. "It's important that we follow the department's process. The matter is being addressed and actively worked on. I recognize the hardships and the frustrations, but I assure you that your case has been flagged, and everything is being done to locate and ameliorate the issues that have stopped your benefits."

You feel like telling him that that word—*ameliorate*—was your own. Even you recognize that the manual and all its preferred forms of communication can sound as though they are something that has been computer generated.

"You weren't even born yet, were you?" A little smirk crosses his face, but it's not one that suggests that he's caught you on something. It is more as if he's just found a missing word that now completes a sentence. He lets his shoulders down. His head is nodding.

"Am I right?"

For once, you wish you had the physical copy of the manual. Not to look up anything, but only to hold it. You, who live alone in your first apartment in such a magnificent city, have never felt so isolated and void of human contact. The physical copy is strength. A kind of companionship that also is weighty with authority. The kind someone like you needs. Because despite its warnings and procedures, you are susceptible to this moment of sympathy and connection. Perhaps it is naivety, but you don't think Michael is being deceptive or intentionally manipulative. And you assume the manual has accounted for this in one form or another, but you don't know what it is or what page it is on; only that he is right, that you weren't born until 1992. And you say . . .

He says . . .

And you say . . .

Don't Let It Kill You

i.

IN THE company of her father and her father's chosen lawyer, Billie held defiant inside the Bureau's interrogation room on Wilshire. This was a railroad job. A total breach of protocol based on hearsay from a neighbor who'd overheard a supposed hushed discussion on New Year's Day between Billie and her four college friends about a plot to kill someone while pretending to hold them for ransom. And how that neighbor had inferred that Governor Reagan was the intended victim (or that there even was an *intended victim!*) was beyond anyone's understanding, other than that the last year or more had been one never-ending uprising, and it seemed that anything must be possible. The responding agents had thanked the neighbor for his assistance. They understood that while one ember was being stamped out, another flame was always rising.

Her lawyer looked across the table. "Evidence? Documented threats? Anything? Why are we all sitting here today?"

With warrants still pending and no arrests made *yet*, the special agent in charge said, "Today is a discussion about what happens when people help each other out."

He explained this was an ongoing investigation, with the focus now having shifted to what they'd uncovered following the initial complaint. Namely that SEWN appeared to be more than a loose-knit student group. Instead, it was an expansive underground network, potentially made up of dozens if not hundreds of small chapters. There was no doubt that SEWN, as a major subversive threat to the United States, was operating at a level of sophistication that extended beyond the means of five suburban college student friends.

Billie reached behind her chair for her sweatshirt. She couldn't shake the chill.

Among the evidence the team had seized, the agents took specific interest in the New Year's Day meeting minutes. In them were indications that Billie had concerns about how SEWN was operating.

Nothing was private anymore.

Billie tucked her hands under her thighs, trying to warm them.

After stating that Billie had the power to decide whether she would exit here as a potential co-conspirator or as a fact witness, the lead turned to her father. "Isn't it better for your little girl to get back to studying American Literature instead of trying to take down America?"

Billie's lawyer coached her not to say anything further. He warned her that the investigators would cling to any word, rearrange the context, and get her so turned around and tangled that she'd end up confirming things she knew to be false. No one would care when she protested over and over to them that *that's not what I meant*. He announced going forward, his client would limit all her answers to *yes*, *no*, or *I don't know*.

The lead agent pushed a photograph across the table. A black and white snapshot whose edges looked as if they'd been overly handled. There they were, the so-called chapter, sitting around the black metal patio table in Peter's parents' backyard at the New Year's Day barbecue, the beginning-of-the-year plenary. In the background, the grill sizzled as the various parents went in and out of the house, returning with platters, trays, and drinks.

Calling it a chapter, much less a network, was a bit generous. Five students who'd met at a potluck two years ago, they christened themselves SEWN—Students for Ending the War Now. And though they were passionate about their message, they couldn't seem to find a voice between SDS, who they found too procedural, and the Weathermen, who they found too violent. Forever at a crossroads of identity, SEWN wasn't interested in controlling political power, inciting violence, or, for that matter, using irreverence to drive home their point. To claim they ever were united or organized by any common operating principle would be a stretch of the imagination.

Maybe that confirmed the Bureau's suspicions?

Billie stared at the photo, at herself, her friends, and the strange conjunction of child's play and adult conviction. A criss-cross shadow pattern from the towering Magnolia netted their collective heads. At the moment the picture was taken, Peter had just finished arguing for some stupid scheme that called for SEWN to publicly claim to have the missing Paul McCartney head, saying it would bring them the necessary attention to make their broadside against the *imperialist war machine*. But, he'd said, to pull it off, they'd need proof of life, at which point Dale asked how you can have proof of life from something that's not alive. That was where the neighbor came in: on the other side of the fence, Mr. Barton, a sub at LAHS, acting like he led a monastic life in his garden when he was nothing other than a snoop. In the picture, Billie saw herself sitting at the edge of the row and side-eying Peter, her lips turned down into a slight scowl, with an arrogance that now made her blush, especially knowing her father could see it too.

"Come on, now, Billie," said the lead agent. "Anyone can tell from this snapshot that you're not comfortable with what's going on. Are you really going to clam up now?"

He was right. She had objected to Peter's plan, saying it violated the SEWN charter and bylaws. Particularly the line that stated that they were not an organization *served by pranks, encouraging and/or participating in the destruction of property, and/or any action that causes harm to any living thing*. But she never took them seriously. Those boys were all talk. Always all talk. A TV version of radicals. Sometimes beautiful and sometimes frustrating, and sometimes even believable.

She couldn't imagine—

But maybe—

Her lawyer had called it climbing the ladder. From your rung, you give up the person on the next rung. And then that person does the same. Up and up and up until they reach the top.

Questions and accusations. Assumptions that she knew something. Around and around and around and around. Who talked with whom, when, and why, and who led what. Through a reconstruction made from the dished-out fragments and pieces, a person could come to believe anything about herself, about the people around her.

Yes, no, I don't know.

Trying to reignite her indignation, she'd asked her lawyer, "But what if there is no up, up there?"

Her father said, "Enough about your friends and protecting them. We're here to take care of you."

ii.

ON THE approach into Tegel, the rising sun makes a silver mirror off the surface of the wing before spilling golden over the scattered buildings of West Berlin.

She hasn't yet moved her watch forward. Back home, it's ten-thirty at night. Here, it is six-thirty in the morning. An early six-thirty.

As the plane taxies to the gate, Billie leans forward and slips on her shoes—canvas tennis shoes pushed deep under the seat in front of her. Everything else she's brought is in a rucksack in the overhead bin. Just enough of her old life to seed the new one.

Stuck in the window seat, she rubs her palms against her burning eyes, nearly elbowing the man beside her in his temple. As the plane taxis, he stares at his knees, running his hands against his denim jeans. Since he sat down in the aisle seat while boarding at her layover in New York, it's bothered her how familiar he looks.

"Sorry," she says.

"Pardon?" he asks. He's clearly American, which she suspected. For most of the flight, he was engrossed in a book that she's been meaning to read; his copy laid flat on the tray table, wide open with the binding broken, as he made notes and marks throughout the margins. He'd only tucked it away into his coat for the descent.

"I just said I was sorry. About the elbow."

"Oh, okay. . . . It's okay."

She says, "Sometimes it takes forever to get off these planes. You get restless."

He nods politely while fingering the pages of his book.

Billie stands partway, her knee on her seat, balancing her elbow against the headrest in front of her. "You know," she says. "This may sound strange, but I keep thinking you look familiar. As if I know you from somewhere."

"It happens sometimes."

He's just under six-foot, with long legs that leave him folded into the seat. His clothes suggest a man in his late twenties dismissing formality—besides his Levi's, he wears a chamois shirt and a brown corduroy jacket. His hair is sandy, slightly shaggy but carefully styled, and one can see the paths from his fingers constantly pushing through its waves. And while his chin cuts maybe a little more angular than most, it softens as it flows upward toward lips that seem kind of feminine, almost oval, and plump. It strikes Billie as strange. The very perfection of him is what makes her feel certain they have met before.

"Maybe from Southern California?"

"Could be." He shrugs, showing no interest in helping her solve her riddle.

"It's just strange. . . . Do you like that book? The one you were reading. It seems like it's the one everyone seems to love these days."

He glances down at the book in his coat pocket, where the top sticks out, pushing up the flap. For a second, his face lights up. "Oh, yeah," he says, nodding. "If you haven't already read it. . ."

"I've been meaning to."

He says she'll be glad she did, and then turns from her, returning his gaze to his knees.

Passengers near the front start to tighten and lean forward. All are waiting for the door to open. The rest of the cabin readies for their exit, grabbing their carry-ons and reaching up for the bins. In wrinkled coats and shirts, they sweep mussed hair off their glassy eyes.

But the familiar man next to her remains seated, showing no urgency to disembark. He even reaches for the inflight magazine, *Lufthansa Bordbuch/Logbook*, with a line map of the globe on the cover, opening it across his lap, and flipping the pages without appearing to read any of them. She's getting the feeling he might have been on TV or in a movie, and he's used to people thinking they know him. That all he wants to do is hide. She can appreciate that.

Billie considers stepping over him. But what's her rush? Yes, after an entire day of flying, getting off this plane would be a relief; but as she finds herself sitting back down, Billie tells herself that just making it to Berlin is the relief. Her parents, eager to get her away from the anti-war troublemakers she'd become mixed up with, pulled strings through Congressman Rees's office to help get her enrolled at Free University mid-year to continue her schooling. She was on edge the whole time at LAX and then JFK, certain that the FBI would send someone to stop her. It's no secret they've continued to watch her. They told her as much would happen, following her interrogation. And while this ordeal isn't over yet, and indeed may only be beginning, at least she has managed to make it this far, into another country, without anyone resisting. Safe and in shared anonymity with a possible movie star.

iii.

Hey, Mr. Barton. Hey, Ray Barton. This isn't Iceland. This isn't the Cold War, and it's not 1952. A coincidence like this one? Would you really swear that's Alla three houses down? This is your lawn, Ray Barton.

Don't let it kill you. Please.

Hey, Mr. Barton. Retired out of Edwards Air Force Base, substitute teaching American history at LAHS, have you really only moved to your bungalow a month ago? Don't be embarrassed at being middle-aged and living alone, Mr. Barton. You can still bring yourself to talk with the neighbors. You don't owe any explanations. So, what if your wife and teenage daughter moved to Santa Clarita after you reported the kids next door to the FBI? Of course, you hated having to turn them in, but what else were you supposed to do? You'd known them since they were born. Good children. But since college, they'd become swept up into the agitating nonsense of college kids you saw every night on the TV news. You know what you heard. It was an obligation. You don't owe any explanations. They were under a spell, and people under spells are the most dangerous of true believers.

Your wife called your actions a symptom, and your daughter called you a tripwire. Both used the phrase *tired of tiptoeing*.

To be honest, Mr. Barton, it doesn't seem as though you're really that crazy about yourself, either.

Let's review: She unloaded her car, grocery bags in the back of a light blue Ford sedan. Her face was hidden by her hair falling forward, veiling her profile. It was the same cut you remember; only the blond had turned a little whiter. The retired man across the street watched you through the picture window. You could feel his opinion forming. Turning away quickly, you didn't want to stare. As sure as you were about seeing Alla, maybe you knew it for what it really was—your mind reordering chapters.

Could it be, Mr. Barton, that since being on your own, it's
been easier to live in the past than to exist in the present, or, even
worse, to think about the future?

Let's pretend this is Iceland. Let's pretend this is the Cold War,
and that it's 1952. You, Mr. Barton, were stationed in our own
little America at Keflavik Air Force Base, known as the Iceland
Defense Force. We'll remember Alla as a local who lived in Keflavik with her parents and brothers, and who worked part-time
in the *Garden Fresh* produce section of the base grocery store.
Barely twenty, if a day. She ran the produce hose over the leafy
greens with such careful attention that you could not have looked
away if you tried. You were surprised when she spoke to you
at length—none of the other Icelanders spoke more than they
needed to. Resentments throughout the island were high, and
people were militant in their resistance to the American creep
into their culture. Alla's voice had been so sweet, her accent clear
and ringing. It was as if she was always waiting for you when you
came in. Someone actually interested in what you had to say.

You must have had some suspicions when she invited you
into town. That was off-limits. A breach of protocol. But you
were young, and you did not yet understand how things could
go wrong. You had not imagined yourself as an intruder. You
thought only of Alla.

Hey, Mr. Barton, was it harder to accept that her brothers
had been lying in wait or that she didn't seem to react when they
attacked you? The next day, bruised and scratched, you wanted to tell her you knew it wasn't her fault. She couldn't be held
responsible for her reactionary brothers. The girl taking Alla's
place at the *Garden Fresh* section shrugged. She tried to act like she
didn't know what you were talking about. Anyone could see how
impossible it was for her to believe it, her own act.

Would you really swear that's Alla three houses down? This is
your lawn, Ray Barton.

Don't let it kill you. Please.

Don't feel lousy, Ray Barton. Those kids can be brutal. No one could cover a review of Shays' Rebellion for Mr. Thompson without taking a lashing from his students. Mr. Thompson is a hero. Those kids worship him for trekking to Canada to evade the government. Imagine that.

But they could've shown some respect when you read aloud your notes from Mr. Thompson's syllabus. It only takes a couple of shit kids to start it, massacring you in front of the others, eating you alive once they figure out that you barely know the material. On top of that, the night before and this morning, your wife kept saying your daughter was too busy to talk. But you could hear her in the background. A whispered plea to her mother, saying she couldn't handle *him* right now. And the response from your wife, *What makes you think I can?*

Don't feel lousy, Ray Barton.

Alla seems to have two teenagers, a boy and a girl, but no husband. She drove the girl to school the other day after she missed the bus. You didn't need to hear the argument as they walked out the door. You knew it by heart.

Don't feel lousy, Ray Barton. From your lawn, just keep a watch out for her.

Alla's boy has his lawn, too. And he tends to it with a push mower that sounds soothing, a slow rhythmic blade, precise shearing. Funny how you both size each other up from your respective plots. But you, you're the bigger one, Mr. Barton. You don't owe any explanations. Haven't you seen him in the hallway once or twice at LAHS? You must have noticed he was blond like his mother and his sister, tall and broad-shouldered like Alla's brothers who chased you down all those years ago.

Mr. Barton, you, of all people, appreciate his good manners when he stops mowing as you come up toward his house. He nods with pursed his lips. Face glistening with sweat. You see, Mr. Barton, you're no threat. When you tell him he does a nice job, he says it's not his choice, *Using a push mower, I mean.* You tell him it's a good thing the lawn is small.

Do you always take in every detail, Mr. Barton? How he dabs
his sleeve against his forehead. How he closes his eyes for a moment as though they might be stinging. How he looks down when
he tells you his mom's not home, *if you're looking for her*. How he
steps back, polite; in a way, gentle. It must make you think of
your daughter, Mr. Barton. Coming and going in the world at
once. Still believing in everything, while quick to trust in nothing.
Some days, all you want is to forget about her and her attitude,
and other days it terrifies you, the whole idea of being forgotten.

But you, Mr. Barton, you just stare when he says he probably
needs to get back to the lawn, that the push mower makes it take
that much longer. You, Mr. Barton, you just stare, waiting for him
to say something else when anyone could see he really just wants
out of this interaction.

After the boy said, *Nice to meet you*, did you notice you hadn't for-
mally met? Even as you said, *Likewise*? Hey, Mr. Barton. Before
you head back to your house, why don't you turn around and ask
about her? You so badly want to. If nothing else, ask her son what
her name is.

We know, Mr. Barton. It's still unimaginable to believe you're
someone who's become impossible to be with, who needed to
be cast away to live alone on a block in an area of town you'd
barely heard of, only protected by your perfect patch of green
lawn. Instead, you want to believe that somehow you've been following along with the plot points, bullheading your way through
conflicts, all in service to landing exactly where you are supposed
to be. Asking Alla's son the question might prove that it isn't by
chance that this series of letdowns dropped you next door to a
woman who only meant to show you her town in 1952. It would
show that you both are the main characters in this story with a
surprise ending.

What matters is that your life is not some tale in which you
messed up and lost the thread.

It is perfect, Mr. Barton. Symmetrical. A gem of narrative
design.

iv.

What Billie Palmer wrote in the FOIPA request (using the sample letter):

FBI
Record/Information Dissemination Section
Attn: FOIPA Request
170 Marcel Drive
Winchester, VA 22602-4843

Dear FOIPA Officer: FBI

This is a request under the Freedom of Information Act.

Date range of request: January 1970 – January 1971

Description of request:

Documents specific to a January 1970 investigation of the student organization, Students for Ending the War Now (SEWN), and its alleged global reach. Investigation centered on a complaint filed on Monday, January 5, 1970, at an event in the former backyard of Paul and Sylvia Rubin, 8621 Airdrome Street, Los Angeles, CA 90035. Subsequent interviews were conducted with Peter Rubin, Dale Stephens, Edward (Eddie) Golden, Clark Lorymple, and Billie Palmer. Main area of interest is a photograph taken at the January 1, 1970, New Year's Day barbeque at the home of Paul and Sylvia Rubin. It is a 4x6 snapshot of said students prior to the investigation, which, it should be noted, was dropped due to lack of evidence and questionable reliability about the witness who reported the alleged crime.

Please search the FBI's indices to the Central Records System for the information responsive to this request related to:

Student Activism (late 1960s – early 1970s); Anti-War Movement:
Student Organizations in the Los Angeles Area; Suspected
National Domestic Terror Organizations; Threats to Governor
Ronald Reagan; Vandalism of Abbey Road billboard on Sun-
set Boulevard, specific to the stolen head of ex-Beatle
Paul McCartney (December 1969).

I am willing to pay up to [$200] for the processing of this
request. Please inform me if the estimated fees will exceed this
limit before processing my request.

I am seeking information for personal use and not for
commercial use.

Thank you for your consideration,

Name: Mrs. Billie Kellerman
PO Box 3385
La Quinta, CA 92253

*What Billie no longer sees when she looks at the reproduced photo of the last
SEWN meeting:*

She does not see them sitting, debating, and planning in Peter's
parents' backyard. She no longer sees Peter, Dale, Clark, and Eddie as individuals—she barely remembers which one is which.
She does not remember whose idea it was to claim responsibility
for Paul McCartney's head. She does not remember if anyone
agreed with her when she told them it was a bad idea. She no longer remembers the smell of the magnolia tree in the backyard on
a warm winter day, when the sun crept over the roof and shone
down on the five of them.

What she does see:

She sees herself, or a form that might be herself, fading off in the corner of the photograph. Her face is in the sun and bleached white; her dark black hair blends into the shadow of the magnolia tree. It is like she is not there at all.

Berlin

i.

ASTRID KNELT over the record cover, a razor blade in hand, with the ruthlessness of a thief about to cut a masterwork out of the frame, or the carelessness of a child trying to draw mustaches on the Mona Lisa. Pressing the blade into the left corner, she pushed down until it broke through the cardboard, tracing an incision that arched like a sine curve—bending up over the white Volkswagen, the streetlamp, the top of the black van, and the bystander, with its final descent in front of John. Then she made one final cut, straight across the bottom of the pedestrian crossing, before she laid down the razor and carefully pinched each edge to lift and remove the Beatles from Abbey Road. For her brother, an instantly recognizable image; for Astrid, a reminder of all the space that was left behind.

The Kreuzberg flat was dark, and every creak coming down the hallway made her stiffen. Over the center of Abbey Road, she stuck a nondescript note that described the details of her day; something too droll to alarm the State Security who monitored the mail flowing from West Berlin into East Berlin. Then, along the crosswalk white, in what looked like doodles, she inscribed the coded language she and her brother had concocted. The message was her plan for liberating his photographs. A way to smuggle them across the border. She was hopeful the authorities wouldn't notice the cipher, knowing their chief concern was to be on the lookout for the import of western currency. Astrid folded her cutout in half and then halved it again so it fit into the addressed envelope. Tucking the packet into her waist, she buttoned her flannel shirt over it and then zipped her parka up to her chin. Taking a deep breath, Astrid walked out of the apartment building, trying to hold on to her determination.

When she reached the post office, Astrid pulled out the envelope, her so-called *Westpaket*, and handed it over the counter, not quite letting go as the clerk took it.

The postal clerk tugged on the envelope, slim and so purposefully simple that the inspectors would know it was not a subterfuge for hiding Deutsche Marks. But Astrid held on. She was tempted to add words of encouragement along the outside margins of the *Westpaket*, telling her brother that the world is spinning at an increasing rate and that eventually the future will catch up to him. Be patient. Listen closely to the songs from the album when you catch them on our radio broadcasts. All the hope is in them. Just be patient, Klaus. But she resisted writing anything, worried it might only serve to draw attention and scrutiny from the Stasi.

When she finally let go of the envelope, she thought that next time she wouldn't just risk sneaking a plan or message on a hacked-up album cover through the post as a *Westpaket*. Instead, she'd take the record itself to one of the viewing areas on her side of the border, cock her arm and let it soar over the Wall.

ii.

THE FREE-SPIRITED, bandana-wearing guy on the beard oil logo was a completely random image. He was no founder. Originally captured among a crowd at a New York City subway station, his face had been isolated, blown up, and cropped from a photo since taken out of circulation. One of the beard oil's founders had seen the now-disappeared print in an exhibition, and, according to the company's website, he'd "zoomed in on him, as though he was 'later me' looking at 'now me.'"

No one knew who the mystery man was. The company set up a blog for people to write about sightings—a forum that seemed absent of earnestness, instead focused on building brand loyalty. Even knowing that, it was hard not to read the posts.

None of this went over well with the photographer's estate.

A German artist of medium significance, Klaus Schreiber's reputation had come from a series of revelatory snapshots of everyday life behind the Berlin Wall, and later for capturing official photos of Paul McCartney on one of his later tours, posing in front of some of the seedier areas of the Reeperbahn in Hamburg where the young and ambitious Beatles had cut their teeth. Five years ago, long relocated to New York with his sister, Schreiber had died unexpectedly and intestate, leaving the probate court to appoint his sister Astrid as the estate's administrator. In the chasm between grief and attending to outstanding debts and logistical details, this unforeseen executor of her brother's legacy found herself fielding requests from galleries, museums, magazines, and editors. A sudden career shift, and a far cry from nursing. It was during that period when one of the owners of the beard oil company contacted Astrid. She'd successfully negotiated the usage fee, but under the impression the image was only meant for a short-term exhibition, not to sell a product, Astrid hadn't understood the need to set any licensing terms. So, after the one-time payment, the beard oil company had free reign to use the isolated frame of the bearded man in perpetuity. Any way they saw fit. She begged them to let her buy them out of the usage fee. It was an honest misunderstanding. She tried to explain how the commercial purpose contradicted her brother's artistic mission; a lifetime of work should not be compromised by her mistake. But they declined every attempt at negotiation. The company was expanding its product line and was in the process of being absorbed by an international conglomerate. Brand identity was an essential part of its growth.

At least she'd held on to the copyright, allowing her to embargo the original photo from any future use or viewing, a minor reparation of her brother's reputation from a momentary dereliction in protecting it.

Standing at the corner of Seventh Avenue and West 19th, just beyond the gallery, they'd only now become aware of how hard the snow was falling. The city busses turned on their headlights. Trucks dropped their plows, making it hard to hear.

The reporter stepped in closer, almost having to yell to be heard. Defending against the wind, she cinched the collar of her down jacket and then tugged her black watch cap down over her ears. A wisp of hair peeked out across her forehead. It was dyed with henna.

"But I know who he is," she said.

Astrid said she wasn't interested. She no longer wished to have any involvement with anything regarding the company and her brother's photo. She spoke flawless English, only some words and syllables occasionally tinged by her accent.

"Those beard people already made a farce of my brother's work."

"We'll expose them. Shame them."

"You talk about how you know who he is. . . . I don't even know who you are."

The reporter explained it again. She'd made it clear in the half-dozen emails she sent that went unanswered. She'd led with it on each voicemail she'd left at the gallery repping Klaus Schreiber's early works. But with patience and confidence, the twenty-three-year-old recent J-School grad said again that she wrote for *40 Steps*, an online publication that believed that any structural injustice could be seen in microcosm within forty steps of anyone's front door; its mission was to shine a light on them and reveal the economic inequalities within our city.

"And this one," she said, "is big."

"I really need to go."

"Please," the reporter said. "I've been waiting out here for . . . Just another minute."

They stepped back underneath the awning. Astrid tried to brush away the snow on her shoulders. But it stuck like part of the fabric.

The reporter continued, saying it was sickening. Everywhere she turned, she saw the logo of the bearded man, the woodcut image of him. In the bins at the checkout line at Whole Foods, posters in the windows of CVS, flyposting on every construction barrier.

"See," the reporter said, pointing across the street. "There's one now. Staring right at us."

Astrid looked down, sliding her boots back and forth through the slush. By this point in her life, she was tired of outrage. Weary of urgency.

"It doesn't bother you how the company has turned finding the so-called bearded man into a contest? Their hefty prize. Their stupid advertising campaign: *'Taking Care of Yourself Shouldn't be the Challenge.'* That doesn't bother you?"

Astrid said she was sorry. But this just wasn't her issue. "I really should go. The train will be a mess."

"A homeless guy," the reporter blurted out. "He used to walk up and down the 1 Train rattling his cup of coins." Her tone hastened, last minute and rushed. "That's who we're talking about. A person. I saw him every day when I went to Columbia. A Vietnam vet always asking for change, saying his benefits have been tangled up for years and years."

"I can tell this is meaningful to you. It's just . . ."

"And now this multinational corporation that owns the beard oil company is making millions off him while he gets nothing? I mean, I'm sorry, but . . ."

"There's nothing I can do."

The reporter said that there was—that's why she was here. If *40 Steps* were allowed to run the original photo, they could subvert the parent corporation's game of identifying the bearded man, publicly calling out the conglomerate for profiting off the homeless man.

A plow growled by, pushing its growing load up Seventh Avenue while kicking up a light spray over the sidewalk. It shone like glitter.

"The photo is out of commission," Astrid confirmed. "For good." The last bit of snow slid off her shoulder, falling in an icy sheet.

Astrid sat at her kitchen table. The misted perfume from a just-peeled orange perked up the grim mid-December morning. By and large, the city remained closed because of yesterday's blizzard.

She ignored the two emails from the *40 Steps* reporter. The first one wanted to know if Astrid had given it more thought, followed by the second that sounded more pleading.

Nothing but funhouse mirrors, Astrid thought. All perceptions shifted and distorted. Despite the noblest of ideals, this young reporter couldn't see she was but one piece caught up in the enterprise of myth perpetuated by the beard oil company. Why not talk about the Paul McCartney Hamburg sessions? Or even the career-defining East Berlin prints? Those works had been far more important.

Astrid deleted the emails. She'd had enough of shame. Almost her whole life had been focused on her older brother and his work. His devotee and his protector. And it all was undone by a stupid mistake. His whole reason for making art wiped away by her carelessness. And now this *40 Steps* reporter was trying to return that shame to her, as though it was Astrid's eternal duty to undo it?

A third email pinged through. And then a fourth.

The pith under the orange peels began crusting and turning color. It started to smell of compost.

iii.

Astrids Checkliste für Billie, den 3. März 1970

√ At the Bahnhof Friedrichstrasse Checkpoint: Pay attention to the direction signs to avoid the slow lane, have US passport ready, buy the daily visa from the guard, exchange the requisite 25 West German marks for the 25 East German marks, and be ready to explain about being an exchange student from the US and that you're only there as a tourist to visit Humboldt University. But don't do any of that as though it's been rehearsed. That would be the giveaway. Fumble a little. Ask for confirmation.

√ Travel with nothing other than the camera case. Contents: a Praktica camera and eight canisters of film. Nothing else should be inside. No passport, visa, money, or receipts inside the camera bag. Keep them in a coat pocket.

√ To the border guard, confirm aloud the policy that photos are not allowed of the police, checkpoints, subways, or the Wall. Ask if it's okay to photograph the iconic buildings that make up the campus. Say that's the only intention.

√ In front of the courtyard at Humboldt, look for Klaus on the stoop under the wrought iron fence, sit beside him, and strike up a conversation.

√ Important: Set down the camera bag next to the identical one he'll be carrying, which will be holding the same Praktica and eight canisters of film. In case the police or Stasi listen in, only talk about the university, about good places to take photos.

√ When he stands to leave, let him "mistakenly" take the "wrong" bag. On the off chance a policeman notices, just laugh about the confusion, noting the coincidence of an identical bag and its contents.

√ After Klaus goes, walk around the campus and photograph the buildings using only the film currently in the camera. Just be natural. And in awe. And then head back to the checkpoint, exchange the East German marks, and cross back into West Berlin.

Klaus' Situation -- Hintergrundinformation (für Billie), den 13. März 1970

√ The original sin belongs to Klaus. It was stupid pride. Once he'd been invited into the Akademie der Künste, the honor of being recognized as a member of the prestigious art academy in East Berlin clouded his judgment. Even before the Wall, he should have known. He should have left.

√ In the East, anything related to art is confined to promoting the state. And that, Klaus knows, is not art.

√ Klaus has no objective of exposing the desolate and frugal state of his city. In the pictures he secretly makes, he is not working to bear witness to the grand oppression. Just the opposite. Despite his situation, he is struck by the simple grace of humanity, the tender way that a small flower can grow in a crack in the pavement. The beauty of perseverance on the faces. Hard architectural lines against a soft and molded sky.

√ In contrast to his artwork, Klaus is very sentimental. Even as a boy, he was always filled with longing and mournfulness. Easily prone to tears.

√ All of his photos remain on the film and spooled in canisters. He has never seen them as they were meant to be seen. They will never survive otherwise.

Billie's Conditions for Astrid, March 14, 1970

Here is one thing you must do -- NEED to do -- before I go: You have to take both of your lists (checklist about your plan, and the next one about your brother's background), burn them in the sink, and then flush them down the toilet. More than anyone, from my past experience with the US authorities, I know the complete sense of helplessness you feel when the ordinary objects of your life are called out as suspicious and suddenly in demand of an accounting.

** Maybe this is obvious, but you should also include this note.

iv.

SITUATED IN front of the iron gate before the main building of Humboldt University, at Unter den Linden 6, Klaus looks as though he's part of a portrait, an illustration ripped from a history book. A breathtaking monument to classicism. Standing on the boulevard, Billie is struck by seeing him at the entryway into this village whose residents have included the likes of Marx, Einstein, Schopenhauer, Hegel, W. E. B. Du Bois, and the Brothers Grimm.

Who needs to *pretend* to be in awe?

Sitting patiently on the stoop, legs crossed, Klaus stares out over the street, almost one among the statuary. His posture, slightly hunched and contained, is amazingly present and alert. It's strange how dissimilar his face is to his sister's. Astrid's is angled and pronounced, as though the product of perfect engineering and design. His features look as though they were drawn on, not quite accurate or proportionate, yet exquisitely sharp and modern, as though revealing a new form of beauty.

Or maybe it isn't him?

Billie hesitates to sit down. Not seeing the camera bag, she walks past him, pausing before the entrance into the courtyard.

She can hear his breathing off to her right, slow and whistling through his nose. He has gotten up to follow her. It takes all her will to resist the urge to acknowledge him.

Billie takes out the Praktica. Acting as though she'll be taking a picture, she aims the lens at the details over the door of the main building and, while focusing it, turns the camera toward the stoop, trying to peek through the viewfinder for a trace of the bag. Instead, she sees a uniformed policeman watching her as he strolls up the boulevard.

Other than the security, very few people are out. The occasional car puttering by sounds like a suggestion. And the breeze gusting up the pavement mostly reminds her of a whisper. It's hard to imagine, but Billie finds comfort in this. After being trailed by FBI agents because of her anti-war activities, she'd learned to be acutely aware of the lingering presence of someone just out of sight. Here, it is a curious relief to see the surveillance apparatus so open and apparent.

Billie puts the camera back into the bag, nestling it against the film canisters. She takes several steps to the side, pretending to look at the sculptures arrayed along the roofline of the U-shaped building. Out of the corner of her eye, she spots the brown leather camera bag, identical to hers. Per the plan, it's on the bench, leaned against his thigh. She tries to conceal any visible sign of relief.

Two weeks earlier, having ducked out of unexpected rain, Billie and Astrid sat in a café, nursing cool cappuccinos and picking at a pastry they split. Astrid explained she always imagined herself coming of age in a Germany with no past. Born three years after the war ended, to her, the previous generation simply didn't exist, beyond ghosts haunting the streets. Their essence, along with their prior convictions, long ago evaporated from this world. Her generation was supposed to be a fresh start. Severing all ties or lineage. And yet, despite those beliefs, that innate understanding, Astrid and her peers still couldn't fathom how it was they'd stepped out of the shadows of the previous generation into a newer shadow.

"Now you, tell me your story again," Astrid said. "I need my little helping of hope."

It was several weeks after they'd first met during a stoppage on the red line, coming back from classes at Free University. Billie, from California, was taking a degree in Comparative Literature, and Astrid studied biology. They'd connected over their shared frustration about the train, quickly broadening their conversation to their view of the world. Since then, they'd gone out for dinner every evening when they commuted together after their late afternoon classes. On weekends they wandered the city. With Astrid serving as a tour guide, they talked politics, professors at FU, The Beatles versus The Rolling Stones, and unreachable boys. This afternoon, as they'd milled about near Bernauer Straße, where people climbed ladders to look over the Wall, hoping to see friends and relatives, Astrid had been especially down about her brother. She'd received a coded letter from him. He was worried his photographs wouldn't survive the Stasi. She needed to find a way to help him.

That was before the rain came.

"Tell me again," Astrid said, leaning across the table.

Billie kicked off her shoes under the table, her socks wet after treading through a puddle. She knew she seemed heroic to Astrid each time she told the story of how she ended up in Germany. It gave Astrid more inspiration to believe she could help her brother and his art.

But today, she didn't feel like reciting the narrative again. It didn't seem right anymore, especially as Astrid struggled with her own situation. Because although the facts were accurate, the context of Billie's story had been exaggerated. She'd never included that it was based on a misunderstanding by the FBI and that she'd never been a true radical; nor how it was her parents who'd paid an arm and a leg to send her to Germany—by no means was she on the lam. In fact, truth be told, she'd been a coward who left her friends behind in the States to fend for themselves.

Astrid waited, rapt, blowing across the coffee before sipping. "Well?"

Billie pinched off the end of her scone and sat back, waving her damp feet under the table. It killed her how much Astrid needed to hear it. She held the pastry like a cigarette. "It was a dark and stormy night . . ."

"First time in East Berlin?" Klaus asks.

"First time, yes."

Seated on the stoop, they speak as though every word will be transcribed and used against them.

He continues to gaze forward, never turning to make eye contact. Partly, she thinks this is from caution due to security. But partly, Billie thinks, he must not want to look at her too closely. She wouldn't want to, in this situation, not when she is free to leave, and he is not. That feeling alone could kill anybody.

"This is a beautiful part of the city," he says. "What is left, that is."

"I can tell."

"You should take more pictures. Many photos. Let others see this city as you are seeing it."

She is supposed to ask him where else she should take photographs and then get up and go with the switched bag. That was the plan. But she doesn't want to leave yet. Who would want to abandon him here? It feels like a step in any direction is a step toward confirming Klaus's fate. If you drive a wedge hard into the crack in the world, you'll only risk loosening a vulnerability.

Another policeman walks by, his long gaze held on them.

"Haus Unter den Linden," Klaus says loudly. "The library. It's still a bit worn from the war, but a wonderful example of Neo-Baroque architecture. You'll want to take your photos before it gets dark." He makes as if he's going to stand, stealthily resting his hand on her camera bag. "It was nice talking with you. Enjoy your visit to East Berlin."

So badly she wants to mention Astrid. So badly she wants to reach down and brush her hand against his.

Heading past the hodgepodge of brutalist construction and classic Prussian architecture, Billie hugs the new camera bag to her side, its deep brown leather one of the few points of color along Unter den Linden. She reaches out and touches each adolescent Linden tree that she passes on her way toward the checkpoint, planted as part of the restoration of the post-war destruction. And for a moment, it's like she's in the outdoor equivalent of a college apartment, furnished in mismatched odds-and-ends and hand-me-downs, and she feels overcome by the resourcefulness of fragility, ingenuity, distress, and make-believe—how it is that we can always manage to find ways to make a home.

She'll remember that feeling the following week when she and Astrid are back at Bernauer Straße. This time Astrid has brought a ladder. She stands on it, urging Billie to come up. The day is clear, with no clouds or fog. Just a crisp and bitter breeze. Perfect for visibility. Atop the second to last rung, leaning slightly forward to balance herself, Astrid rests her palms against the shelf.

"Hurry," she says. "Hurry."

People are scattered, also elevated, some hugging the streetlamps, others braced against the road signs. Several wave white handkerchiefs, hoping to distinguish themselves to friends and family gathered on the other side of the Wall. It's a good idea, having a signal, one that hadn't occurred to either of them until they got there.

She'll remember that feeling when Astrid calls down to her, "I see Klaus. . . . Come, come, come. Now. I see him! The back of his head. He's looking around." Then Astrid unzips the top of her parka and unwinds her lavender scarf from around her neck. Bunching it up, she begins waving the loose ends above her head, trying to get his attention.

"Hurry, hurry, hurry."

The ladder shakes, only steadying once Billie finally steps onto it.

v.

JUST YESTERDAY, Michael Bennet, an until-recently homeless Vietnam Vet in New York, started seeing his image everywhere in drugstore windows and on subway ads. At first, Michael thought he was imagining it. But there it was again, over and over, staring back at him, disembodied and intent. He tried taking different routes. But as he turned each new corner, Michael saw it again. It made no sense. He'd been taking his meds. Doing well by all accounts. A new job. A place to live. He'd been checking in regularly with the social worker, dedicated to being straight with her about everything. But everywhere he turned, it haunted him, his own face staring back at him. He couldn't get off the streets fast enough. Once Michael got back to his studio apartment, he turned the lock and propped a kitchen chair against the door. He pulled the curtains shut and covered the bathroom mirror in long strips of masking tape. Sitting on the corner of his bed, his back braced against the wall and a pillow in his lap, Michael Bennet stayed up all night, willing away tomorrow, terrified that to be out meant facing more hallucinations, his own head trailing him in windows all over the city.

The Unclaimed

i.

THE PREOCCUPATION took hold when the woman who would become my wife pointed behind her and said that she thought Ray Charles lived somewhere up there in those hills. We weren't regulars on the south side, so we approached each visit like tourists. She was referring to View Park, a part of town known as the Black Beverly Hills. It was only on her mind, she said, because she'd just read about it somewhere; knowing her, probably in the *Freep*. It was just a comment. An observation.

Who knew Renaldo actually was listening to us.

We'd been talking as though he wasn't there, she and I. Sitting out in the backyard of his group home in Baldwin Hills, on the same side of a faded wooden picnic table without an umbrella, we were shaded by a sweeping canopy of a tree we couldn't name. It made me think of my childhood, how the smell of the little white blossoms was more a part of me than I might have imagined.

Being there was an obligation. We'd been coming to the group home since the moment we'd learned what had happened. While reporting for a local weekly on the protests at People's Park up north in Berkeley, Renaldo had taken one right across the skull, a policeman's billy club, and after a month in a coma, he awoke as a four-year-old living in a grown body. We wanted to offer some familiarity. Renaldo had once been a good friend. He would have done the same for either one of us.

Renaldo claimed the same spot he did each time we visited, at the very edge of the opposite bench, as if he were ensuring he could escape at a moment's notice. As we made small talk, you could see him drifting into his own head. His lips began to move. Working something out. That's when we turned to talk among ourselves, figuring it was being here that was the most important part, the connection.

He started really going at it after she mentioned the house. *Ray Charles's house. Ray Charles's house.* A mutter turned into a yell. *Ray Charles's house. Ray Charles's house.* Each word carefully delineated and pronounced, somewhere between a protest chant and a soothing mantra.

The staff peeked through the windows, pulling aside the curtain to make sure they were seen. They let him carry on, figuring it made no difference. You could tell they hoped it would pass. It was near lunchtime.

Man, did he start jawing.

The staff started to mobilize once Renaldo stood up. *Ray Charles's house. Ray Charles's house.* And then he got stuck in place, his legs and ankles tangled in the bench's bracing. The table started rocking while he worked to free himself, frustrating him to a degree we'd never seen.

We jumped up and backed away. By then, three staff had already descended from the house, triangulating and approaching him like he was wounded and unpredictable game. One of them, a man with a stubbornly large forehead, kept waving at us. *Go now*, he said, unwilling to make eye contact. *Go. Now.*

You've got to engage, man, Renaldo liked to say when we were all undergrads at UCLA. *Become part of the moment, not just be a witness to the moment.* He had so much integrity, Renaldo. It hurt you to look at him, in part because it could make you feel lousy for the corners you cut, the willingness to bend toward complicity or conformity out of ease. While we were screwing around with "finding ourselves," some of us traipsing through an endless series of failures, his life was a focused search for truth and the restoration of dignity to those who'd been oppressed. Maybe that's why it was so hard to see him in this new state and why we were never quite willing to fully accept the extent of the damage from the injury.

But there were actual moments, seated at that table in the backyard of the group home, when Renaldo, out of the blue, would drift into lucidity. Where sometimes, just for a moment, in maybe a sentence or two, you could sense the real him, and it was like he was reaching out, calling out, to let you know he was still inside of this mangled version of his brain, still searching for truth and justice, and still the same person he always was.

The woman who would become my wife once got furious when I pondered if this were wishful thinking on our part.

We got a call from the Residential Director at the group home saying that *this Ray Charles House issue* only flares up in our presence and that it lingers for days after we leave. It unnecessarily burdens her staff.

She said that until they could figure out how to redirect Renaldo and his fixation on this topic, she didn't think we should visit—that is, unless we had some ideas.

Now it was our responsibility. As if we were the experts.

Later that week, Renaldo went missing. His bed was made, the pillows fluffed. His house slippers were lined up perfectly under the locked window. It was unclear how he got out. Apparently, no one noticed until lunch. The staff scrambled, searching through the home, looking behind all the shower curtains, peeking under the beds, and throwing open closet doors. The whole household temporarily collapsed in disarray, with most of the residents worked up and panicked by the mysterious urgency. Within twenty minutes of being called, the cops found him trekking along South La Brea, moving past the oil fields in the direction of View Park, the neighborhood where Ray Charles lived. He didn't put up any resistance. When the cruiser pulled up, Renaldo walked over in compliance and tried to open the locked back door, grasping at the handle, knowing it was time to go back. He's lucky they didn't shoot him.

That we were not welcome back was made official in a polite but ominous letter from an attorney. It came within three business days of Renaldo's sojourn to find Ray Charles's house, filled with terms like *complainant, guardian ad litem, gross negligence, liability, trespasser,* and *undue influence.* The claim was that this letter came at the request of Renaldo's family, although later we'd learn from his sister that they weren't even aware there had been any problems until they were informed he was being moved hundreds of miles away to an institution in the Central Valley, offering the minimal evaluation: *He is not prepared for this level of living nor an urban environment, both of which encourage inappropriate behaviors.*

Later records obtained by the family for a civil suit showed something a little more precise about Renaldo's final days in Baldwin Hills. An unsealed internal report documented that he'd been asking for us, over and over. Every morning he'd eat breakfast and wait by the door. *When are they coming?* He'd ask. *When are they coming?* He refused all activities for fear of missing our arrival. Each day, the staff said we wouldn't be there. *When are they coming?* He'd ask. *When are they coming?* Finally, after a few days of this, in a pique of frustration, the manager-on-duty told him we were never coming and that we were never allowed on the property again. Ever. The report noted that when given this news *resident displayed belligerence.*

But even that, it turns out, was not what prompted the hastened relocation. It was a small act. One of defiance. One of loyalty. One found by the Residential Director on the floor in the center of her office, a pile of freshly laid defecation, accompanied by a note, neatly written with model penmanship: *You shit on my friends, I shit on your floor.*

When we learned of this long after the fact, the woman who would become my wife asked me if I still believed it was wishful thinking. That is, that the semi-familiar body we'd been visiting indeed was only giving shelter to Renaldo, as we'd known him. When she put it that way, I could only picture Jonah holed up in that whale, suffering inside the giant mammal, hanging onto its rib cage for survival when the salty waters rushed in, questioning himself and his own sense of futility and purpose, fading and fading until God spoke up on his behalf and Jonah was spat out from the intestinal cavity onto the shore, given the chance to earn redemption.

She asked, "Is it possible you're conflating it with Pinocchio?"

I paused and considered. I really wasn't sure. It was only later, after her diagnosis, that I began to really understand this very conversation and how it must feel to know the waters rushing in.

ii.

SOMETHING ABOUT a division called the Office of the Unclaimed Dead infiltrated our thinking. And though we are women and men of science and of logic, of evidence and reason, of propositions and of tests, of Aristotle and Descartes, and even though we'd recently moved into the twenty-first century, somehow we were willing to entertain a supernatural explanation.

In 2003, initially in Los Angeles, Monty's face started showing up as stenciled images on alley walls. And then as little stickers surreptitiously and strategically plastered on billboards advertising corporate products. It wasn't clear whether it was protest, commentary, or just a form of playful vandalism. Nobody knew who put them up. The images just appeared. Even the middle-of-the-night security guards never witnessed anything. One moment there was nothing; turn around, and there they were. It made local news and then national news. Soon they were in Northern California, and then they started showing up in New York and parts of New England. Everywhere we happened to live. A kind of public art movement.

There were no manifestos. No statements. The silence of their creator only suggested deeper meaning and purpose. But despite ongoing speculation—mischievousness, political dissent, a public condemnation of the Supreme Court's installation of George Bush into the White House—the answer was only in people's imaginations.

Not that we knew the answer, either. But here's what we did know: the image. Its exact origin. And it was shocking to revisit it forty years later. We'd been there when the original picture was taken in a little bungalow in Los Feliz. An Instamatic that had been passed around. We could even tell you the exact night. What was served at the Thursday potluck. The stupid things we talked about. We were just kids then. And we knew the face was our old and once-troubled friend Monty, not long after he'd straightened out, and not long before he was found dead under mysterious circumstances. And we also knew that his girlfriend at the time, Sharon, had taken his death hard, and following a psychotic break, had landed in a facility, coping through a variety of treatments, most memorably an art therapy project that produced an endless re-creation of Monty, all based on this very image that suddenly, out of the blue, was showing up everywhere.

Could she?

We wondered, ourselves.

But even with our magical thinking, this seemed beyond her.

She'd been picked up off the street in the early nineties, charged with vagrancy for sleeping in the park. That was in San Francisco, and that was during Matrix, Mayor Frank Jordan's initiative to cleanse the city of the homeless, believing that as a deterrent, he could ticket and fine them for so-called quality-of-life issues. You could pay the forfeiture, appear at a pending court date, or better yet, leave town, none of which Sharon ever did.

Six months later, Sharon had been declared deceased and turned over to the aforementioned Office of the Unclaimed Dead. Found in a hidden pool of mud out near Funston Beach, her body was unrecognizable and bloated, presumed to have been relinquished and abandoned at some point during a long stretch of the beach's closure. Determined to be indigent, finding her triggered no alarms, only a mechanism of bureaucracy. With no identification, her fingerprints were taken, her description matched against reports of those who were missing or fugitives, and a general description was circulated among various police departments and databases. But nothing turned up, leaving Sharon as Jane Doe. Following protocol, as someone declared unclaimed, she was buried at sea, a Bay Area indigent's send-off. Over a year later, her brother, in his on-again, off-again search for her, contacted the city. He had her records from Metropolitan State Hospital. There were copies of her fingerprints in that file, eventually matched to the unclaimed Jane Doe from Funston Beach. He was furious. How could that have been missed? Where was the dignity? She'd once been an assistant teacher at a kindergarten. A daughter. A sister. She'd been denied a family service. The Office of the Unclaimed Dead said they hadn't been aware she had a brother. No one had come forward.

At its most metaphorical, it made sense. We'd been haunted by what happened to Sharon for nearly forty years. Especially Vickie, who forever believed that she'd done in Sharon, not just by capitulating to the police questioning, but by her subsequent inability to accept a gift from Sharon some years later when she visited her at the State hospital in Norwalk.

The fact that the gift had contained the very image of Monty that we were now seeing seemed almost too perfect. We wondered if, perhaps, Vickie was the originator of the stenciled image. Someone had to be, but on consideration, Vickie made for a poor suspect. Vickie had a better reason than any of us to leave the past in the past; being the one who had taken the direct blow. The one who knew the specific moment of failure.

It felt as though someone was fixing our mistakes, remembering the things we had tried so hard to forget. We knew we'd been selfish. Whenever bad things happened to each one of us, as they did, we accepted them as penance for that time in our lives when we might have been so much more courageous.

The dead are the dead—despite an office that tries to lay claim to them by giving them unclaimed status.

The Monty images are the Monty images.

Neither can nor should be confused with the other.

As for the artworks, all we can say is that they brought joy and surprise and curiosity to a cultural moment that seemed to need it, so beaten down by its own unfulfilled illusions, its constant letdowns, and its craving for reasons to believe. How the work got there, through whatever force or human hand, does not change that fact.

Maybe that is too much to assign to a sticker or a stenciled image? It certainly was too much to assign to Monty. And way too much for Sharon. But for now, as an image, it seemed like a total gift.

And yet . . .

Still . . .

You want an answer: Who was it? What was it?

Here's your answer: Mercy. Humanity.

iii.

WITH THE toe of his slipper, the boy pushes open his bedroom door, pausing in the threshold to see if that was Tom who just left his mother's room. Behind him, his mom sits on the floor, cross-legged with a deflated air mattress across her lap, taking deep inhalations and then blowing into the plastic valve pinched between her fingers. With Tom and Julieta commandeering her bedroom, she's been forced to sleep in the boy's room later tonight.

The boy tells her he's off to brush his teeth. It's his best excuse. She wouldn't approve otherwise.

In each hand, he grips a car. The right holds the black Rolls Royce Phantom. In the left, the Mustang Fastback. The leaders of the search team. He just wants to talk to Tom. He's pretty sure he's in the kitchen. Tom's feet always seem to slap the ground when he walks.

The boy peers around the door into the darkening hallway, keeping perfectly still, first scanning the closed door of his mother's room and then, moving right, settling his gaze on the empty living room.

Layers of darkness mix with a seeping luminescence from the streetlamps. Slowly, the furniture starts to take shape. The couch, a bunched-up blanket and a pillow at the bottom. Coffee table and recliner. The hi-fi in the corner and its accompanying milk crate full of LPs. The standing lamp with its slouching shade in front of the bookshelf pushed against the far wall, five shelves of mismatched spines, low and high, like a series of downtown cityscapes at dawn.

He only wants a second with Tom, a chance to confirm that Tom really saw the Paul McCartney head up in the hills. Tom had mentioned it in the morning, but the rest of his story was interrupted. Since then, the boy hasn't seen Tom, sequestered all day and evening in his mom's bedroom with Julieta, only the occasional dash to and from the bathroom. He only wants affirmation from Tom because he, the boy, has begun doubting his own memory of the Paul McCartney head gliding up Sunset Strip. He's lost the details. The most he remembers is a sensation of something deep inside of him floating away.

His mom now kneels over the foot of the inflated air mattress, trying to wrap a fitted sheet under its corners. The pulsing rhythm of her breath has the perfection of industrial machinery.

Hearing noises coming from the kitchen, the boy takes a cautious step out of his room. Instantly, he's greeted by a smell that does not belong to his family. It's something smoky. A little burnt. He moves down the hallway toward the bathroom, staying as far away as he can from his mom's bedroom door. Julieta scares him.

Standing in the bathroom doorway, the boy leans toward the kitchen. His hands squeeze the cars, cutting into his palms.

"Tom?" he whispers. "Tom?" Each utterance is like the wide beam of a flashlight trying to focus itself.

From the kitchen area come more clumsy sounds that are strangely intimate. A sniffle. Groans and mumbled narration. Those usually only made by the unobserved.

"Tom?" the boy tries again, whispering louder, but cautious not to attract his mom's attention. "Tom."

Out of the kitchen darts the shadow that is Julieta. She appears in the hallway, a plate of toast in her hand, momentarily making eye contact with the boy before scampering into the bedroom, slamming the door, and twisting the lock.

Tucking her son in, his mother leans over and kisses him on the forehead and then whispers goodnight. She tugs the gold bedspread just below his chin.

Beside his bed, the air mattress is made, the top sheet neatly curled back, a clean edge over the knit tartan blanket. On the side nearest the door, straddling the gap between two pine floor panels, a candle wobbles in its little brass holder each time his mom moves. Eventually she'll light it, when her son falls asleep. There still are papers to grade. And reading the final chapter of the novel she's been pushing through.

As his mom turns to leave, the boy reaches out and takes her hand, gripping it as though he might otherwise float away. He asks if she remembers what they saw on Sunset the other day.

She says, "What we saw?"

He doesn't want to say *the Paul McCartney head*. It's too spooky to be said aloud.

She sits down on the edge of the bed. The unlit candle on the floor teeters and jiggles. She asks, "Did I hear you talking to someone when you went to brush your teeth?"

He shakes his head. It's a technicality, since there wasn't really any talking. And he's not about to bring up seeing Julieta before going to sleep.

"But do you remember on Sunset?" he asks again. "The people dancing, the crowd?"

Narrowing her eyes, it's as if she's trying to read a transcript of her own memory.

How could she not remember?

She says, "Give me a little more to go on."

He feels light. Airless. Like when you close your eyes at night and you realize how easy it could be to vanish.

"Last Saturday?" she asks. "Is that when we were there?"

"We went out to eat. At Ben Frank's."

"And then we walked around, right? Looked at the *Abbey Road* billboard. It was crowded. So many people jamming the sidewalks. Didn't we just want to get out of there? That's what I remember. Wanting to get away. Was there something else?"

"I guess not," he says, suppressing a yawn. So sleepy.

She rises and pulls the cover up again. "Lights out," she says. "It's been a long couple of days. And tomorrow is school. For both of us." She steps over the air mattress toward the door, causing the unlit candle to tumble backward into the makeshift bed. She says she'll just be in the next room for a while.

Pausing in the doorway, she tells him to go to sleep. "And always remember this: you're perfectly safe in your own house. It is *your* house." He can tell she is saying it loud enough that it will carry into the next room.

"Goodnight," he whispers.

She closes the door all the way, leaving his room so dark, darker than when he closes his eyes.

For just a moment, an intense loneliness overwhelms him. As though his world has just contracted. He's never imagined a life without the two of them before, the boy and his mom. But for just this second, a split-second really, it hits him in a way like nothing ever has, alone and estranged from the rest of the world.

There is nothing in the dark that isn't there in the light. That's what the boy has always been told when he's gotten antsy and afraid at bedtime. And maybe that is true. But it's also true that there are sounds that can only be heard in the darkness, invisible to the ear in full light.

With a last burst of energy, the boy pushes back the covers and climbs out of bed. He inches along the narrow space between his bed and the air mattress, high on his tiptoes to avoid making any noise.

He hears his mom's footsteps treading through the living room. The springs on the couch catching her weight. A rustling of papers followed by a long sigh. And once it quiets down, when barely he hears the pages flipping, there is a clicking from her bedroom door, followed by a scatter to the bathroom, a flush, and then the door shutting with a sharp precision, a stealthiness so understated that he wonders if his mom even has noticed.

Reaching his dresser, where the Dinky cars are parked under the cutout on the bottom, he bends down, patting his hands on the floor until he recognizes the black Rolls Royce Phantom and the Mustang Fastback. Speaking on behalf of the Rolls Royce driver, he asks, *Any luck on the Paul McCartney head yet?* The Mustang driver answers back, *We'll continue searching in the morning. Don't worry. We will locate it. We know it's out here somewhere.*

The boy scoops up both cars. He doesn't need Tom. He knows what he saw.

Ferrying the search team back to his bed, the boy pauses and arches forward over the air mattress, stretching his hand out to the doorknob. With the tips of his fingers, he turns the knob slowly enough to mask the click and then pulls the door open a crack, just enough so that a wave of light rushes through. The knocked-over candle rolls side-to-side, like a stuck secondhand.

iv.

A TRUE story Cassandra likes to tell: "When we were teenagers, my friend and I"—Cassandra means Michael, but she never says Michael's name when she tells this story because to do so would be to sully him, somehow—"were walking to see Robert Barry's *Closed Gallery* show at the Eugenia Butler, you remember, the gallery of La Cienega and Melrose. He actually, and I mean *actually*, slipped on a banana peel someone had trashed on the sidewalk. After my friend got his balance back, he just looked over at me.

They're not kidding about that, he said. And then we kept walking, avoiding our realization that we were living in a boobytrapped world."

V.

HEY, AMY BARTON, this is no way to celebrate your fortieth birthday. At sixteen, you made a promise to yourself that by this age you would make sure your absent father knew how terrible he'd been. With each passing year, the idea of shaming him started to turn closer to forgiving him. Now, moments away from seeing your father for the first time since who knows when, it's all starting to seem pointless. He no longer knows who anyone is, your father.

Blame or forgiveness? You once wondered what you actually would do when the time came. Now it's too late, Amy Barton. To choose either path would be to choose unloading. Cathartic at best. You'd be the *bad guy*.

Don't let it kill you. Please.

Stepping out of the car into the oppressive wine country heat, you can barely bring yourself to say anything to your sometime boyfriend Terry, who earlier announced he'd wait out front, glued to the radio for updates on the O.J. Simpson murder saga, having spent the entire six-hour drive northward toggling between AM radio stations when reception faded and crackled over the Grapevine and through the spray of Central Valley towns. When you look back at him, Amy Barton, you hear the engine of the red sporty rental running, you see the cranked A/C blowing his bangs off to the side. His attempts at recaptured youth are ridiculous. *Lame*, you allow yourself to say out loud, but only where nobody can hear.

On this of all days, the day of your fortieth birthday, walking the cracked concrete path up to the facility door, how is it that, even incapacitated, your father still can manage to pin you down?

Don't feel lousy, Amy Barton. Being in the same region as your father is only a result of a coincidence. Another ridiculous middle-aged moment: a Napa Valley wedding, one in which the bride, your friend, and the groom would be marrying for the second and third times respectively, while insisting the occasion carry the pomp and pageantry of a fairytale wedding. The fact that you were recruited to be a bridesmaid sounded laughable when your friend said it aloud. But you capitulated, years of friendship and exchanged favors, and you dragged Terry along for no other reason than you couldn't imagine doing any of this alone. With the wedding being held in Calistoga, that meant you could visit your father at the VA Hospital in nearby Yountville. Geography no longer was an excuse. Still, you resisted. Terry encouraged you, pulling out the word *closure* from his O.J. murder phrasebook. You said under no circumstances, and that was that. Nothing to talk about anymore. But it ate at you, Amy Barton, something you couldn't justify not doing, despite your well-cultivated collection of rationales and excuses.

Hey, Amy Barton, when your father scoots in, covering his mouth out of caution, and says, "Get me out of here," you must shudder as the decades of resentments come in conflict with your core belief in dignity. You can forgive that he only speaks of himself without saying anything about your birthday; after all, he doesn't even recognize you as his daughter. You don't let it kill you.

Side-by-side, you sit among a half-circle of folding chairs in the common room of the VA's so-called memory care wing, a euphemism which oddly is less comforting than its intended effect. Muzak versions of the Great American Songbook play in the background. From your angle, his once commanding physique has become reduced to its most basic anatomical shell, and his once attentive eyes now droop watery, lost in a semi-permanent haze. Doesn't he look so helpless, Amy Barton? So dependent?

"Please," he whispers. "Get me out of here."

And at that moment, you feel your throat tighten, your intestines squeezing, and it's hard to breathe. This room, meant to be welcoming, has turned stuffy and confining. Each resident who passes by leaves their own unique smell of a body slowly changing form, a distinctive odor of decay that regular showers and disinfectant can't hide.

"Please," he whispers. "Get me out of here."

This man who had held such sway over you, who caused so much embarrassment and humiliation with his pathetic bursts of anger and need to control, now counts on you. He's a one-line hostage note. He whispers his refrain again, his hand over his mouth to shield his words from the passing attendant. All you see, dangling from his wrist, is the beaded bracelet strung with the three block letters that spell out his name (*R-A-Y*), something that causes the attendant, clearly attuned to your expressions, to step in and share that the band was made during arts and crafts, and then, redirecting, she asks if you'll be staying for the sing-along circle.

Let's review: The last straw was the incident when your father reported the neighbor kids as potential threats to America, though in truth, it was not the principle of the thing but the aftereffects that drove you away. The pouting when he was questioned by your mother. The irritation at what he termed your *insolence*. Ranting about the conspiracy of you and your mother ganging up on him. And then just as suddenly checking out, closing the door of his study, sometimes for entire days, retreating into his army scrapbooks, only emerging to sound off at anything he perceived as upsetting the system of his household.

You and your mom moved north to Santa Clarita, hot and dry and rural, while your father stayed in the city, took up in a tiny bungalow, living off a substitute teacher's salary and his military benefits, slowly constricting the financial support he'd once promised.

Your pivot to forgiveness began when you first started teaching middle school. A detour toward empathy. For a spell, you understood confronting a world of frustration. An underfunded district, a room full of adolescents who were there because they were required to be, kids caught with weapons—knives of all sizes, small clubs, razors, and even an occasional gun—who would show them inconspicuously when they wanted to inspire fear, who would grab your arms when they were frustrated and leave bruises and marks, leaning forward and talking so closely that you could feel their spit on your face. And let's not forget the endless meetings about attendance policies, assessments, budget cuts, promoting failing students, rubrics, textbooks, first-period gym versus fourth-period gym, measurable outcomes, onsite police security, detention, bus duty, parent night, budget cuts, copying costs, forced bussing, and lunch duty, and one-to-one conferences, and on and on and on. You too were in shit moods at the ends of the days. You too felt like a live wire at all moments.

Part of you thinks you should still say something even if he won't understand. But intuitively you know that it's a little like the problem with love: putting it out without having it received rarely makes anyone feel as though they've actually loved.

Hey, Amy Barton, why can't your father look at you? Why does he gaze outward when he talks? And why does he start calling you Alla when he asks you to get him *out of here*? Curiously, it doesn't wound you. That's the kind of thing that used to kill you.

Doesn't he look so helpless, Amy Barton? So dependent?

You stand and direct your apologies, your excuses, to the attendant for having to leave so quickly. In a clumsy and formal attempt to sound caring, you say that your schedule does not allow for the sing-along circle. There's a wedding. A rehearsal dinner, you explain. You're a bridesmaid, you elaborate, exchanging embarrassment for faux earnestness. And you keep checking your watch, not that it matters, but somehow as if that is evidence entered on behalf of your itinerary. You stand to leave, thanking the attendant for all she does, forgetting to look at your father. You claim you'll be back. You even repeat that, Amy Barton, as though the repetition is confirmation of your intention. And the attendant says she'll walk you out. Her expression is serious. Near the front door, she says many people find it difficult to see. Especially the first time. She says your father may not know who you are, but he knows you can be trusted, which, the attendant theorizes, means that somewhere inside he does still know you. It will get better with each subsequent visit, she says. Why, Amy Barton, why does that make you feel even more horrible?

This is your fortieth birthday, the expiration date of a declaration you made to yourself a quarter of a century ago. And here you are, seeing your father sitting slightly stooped, his feet tapping, hands shaking, terrified that you'll leave him here alone. It's as though his inner consciousness is exposed like a raw nerve. When it comes to dealing with your father, you've always been caught between having nothing to say and being afraid of what you might say. On this, the day of your birthday, it turns out that the perfect gift is the ability to silently walk away.

Why hurry, Amy Barton? Take it slow. There is no rush to get to the rehearsal dinner.

Walk slowly and take your time. Let Terry wait in the car, absorbed in his talk radio world.

Walk slowly through the sterile hallways decorated by giant photos of vineyards.

Walk slowly and tear the name tag off your blouse, folding the adhesive in on itself before dropping it into a garbage can.

Walk slowly past worried families. Past guards. Past staff digging through their pockets for their cigarettes.

Walk slowly as you leave the building, whose doors magically open for you.

Walk slowly with the realization that your life has not always been a chaotic mess, rather, one in which you've only been following along with the plot points.

Moments ago, while still inside in the ward, you looked back at your father for one last time (so helpless, so dependent). You understood the world was small and that it was scripted, and the conflicts laid out at the beginning always find some form of resolution by the end.

It is perfect, Amy Barton. Symmetrical.

Vanessa

i.

AT JUST past 9:30 at night, almost simultaneously, my friend Tom and I receive emails informing us that a mutual friend named Vanessa has died. This is how it works in the twenty-first century; I'd done the same last year when I had my own news to share. But here's the crazy thing: it turns out Vanessa passed nearly seven months ago, and it is only because another acquaintance ran into her sister that the news of her death reaches us. I guess it goes to the weight of the word *friend* in mutual friend. There is no explanation given, other than that Vanessa ran with the wrong crowd and eventually it caught up with her. The sister told our friend that Vanessa finally is at peace now.

What else could she believe?

By midnight, Tom phones me. He says he can't get to sleep. He asks, "How long has it been?"

Truth be told, I figure it's been more than twenty years since I last saw Vanessa.

Tom figures it about the same, maybe a little less. He can't really say.

Regardless, neither of us even can remember her last name. Still, the news really hits us. Trying to piece together the past is like to trying to remember plots from old TV shows. Who would ever really want to endure them again just to get the answers? But here's what I do remember: Vanessa played an outsized role in my social life for a few years at the close of the sixties—not because we were particularly close, but because Vanessa knew so many people. Being around her for any length of time naturally threw all kinds of people into your orbit. I had met the woman who would become my wife in just such a way, and in time we met Tom, though that was a few years later, after things quieted down for all of us. And that was just what we always liked about Tom: he seemed so detached from the fear and paranoia that was settling in amongst that group of people, our friends, as though he were observing it from a safe remove.

In a manner that I'm long accustomed to after several decades, Tom instructs me to drop whatever I have planned for the morning—he'll be picking me up at a little before ten; we can carry on then. This kind of insistence has become more and more frequent over the past year since losing the woman who became my wife.

He adds, "It's good to have something ahead of you."

After I agree, he yawns. It sounds satisfying. Before hanging up, my friend Tom does something he's rarely done since I've known him. He confesses. He says that he used to be what he calls a Nervous Christian type—that for years he would lay awake worrying about what if there really wasn't a heaven, that when we died we were done and over with. Now, he says, he lies awake worrying about what if there *is* a heaven.

Strolling just ahead of me down the aisle of a box store on West Pico that's rumored to be going out of business, my friend Tom continues his months-long search for a new toaster. He has a *Consumer Reports* rolled up and tucked under his arm, an issue not specific to toasters, per se, but to *the kitchen appliance*. As a general rule, he trades in logic, my friend Tom, living his life based on developing hypotheses and testing his propositions before making any kind of judgment or decision.

This trickles down even to buying a new toaster.

"This," I ask, "is 'having something ahead of you'?"

Tom says he needs a toaster that cooks evenly. He explains the last three he's owned have toasted the bread randomly. Sometimes burnt. Sometimes undercooked. And most of the time a little bit of both, factoring in the two sides of the slice. "It shouldn't be that difficult," he says.

We marvel that there are so many options here.

"Imagine," Tom says, "it wasn't that long ago when we couldn't get a decent bagel in the valley."

"Nor gelato," I add.

Sometimes we like to congratulate ourselves on how the years have made us such sophisticates.

"Three o'clock," Tom says, his voice dropped to an urgent whisper. "Three o'clock."

Just over my shoulder, a salesman is making his way toward us. We are standing dead under the sign hanging from the ceiling that reads SMALL APPLIANCES.

The salesman is a boy, by our standards. It is no wonder the chain is rumored to be going out of business. He has dress pants that hang too low around his pole of a waist, cinched by a belt so tight that he must have had to notch another hole through the leather end just to get it to hold. His white shirt blooms at the rib cage, and though it is tucked in, it is crooked, making everything about him seem slightly off-kilter and out of proportion. There is an earnestness in his eyes. He really is trying to be helpful. But we're having trouble accepting it as such. It's how we are. Or, at this stage of life, how we've become.

But it is the way he speaks that takes all our attention. His literal manner of speaking. At first, we think it is clowny. Short bursts with exaggerated hand gestures. Amplified facial expressions meant to act out his words, as opposed to accompanying them. It's when he says the word *gentlemen* (as in "Good day, gentlemen"), slurring the *n*, the *t*, and the *l* into a single sound that gets caged and stuck in his mouth, that we realize he is hard of hearing. He is unapologetic about the time it takes to form each spoken word, slowly and meticulously, as though he is inventing language on the spot. In a way, we feel embarrassed—initially for him but soon for us, because we feel uncomfortable over something for which we have no reason to feel uncomfortable.

It's unspoken most of the time, but my friend Tom and I share a fear both of how things could have been and how, with just the right circumstance, they still could be. Once, dozens of years ago, I read about a man killed in his living room chair while watching TV. An airplane had blown up in the sky hundreds of miles away, but one little piece of mechanical debris had hurled through the atmosphere, rocketing forever in the direction of his house. It broke through the top pane of the living room window and then hit the man bullseye in the temple. The metal object was the size of a Kennedy fifty-cent piece, made powerful by its flight. It took investigators a while to find it and piece the story together. We're always putting ourselves in those shoes, my friend Tom and I. Be it an unidentified object sailing through the air, or not being able to hear. We don't think we're heroic enough to handle such things.

After the salesman leaves, Tom is holding the toaster that was recommended. So, my friend Tom wants to know, should he buy it? He is uncharacteristically uncertain. He isn't looking at me while he talks. Instead, his eyes are trained on the toaster. He says, "Buying it because the salesman is deaf is no reason to buy it."

Looking at the box, I tell him it does have a top rating: the gold seal of approval. That that confirmation seems legit. The question is if you trust in approbations. And then I correct him: "By the way," I say, "it's *hard of hearing*. He's not deaf. Hard of hearing."

Tom stares a little longer at the appliance. Then he shifts his glance to me, proving that when it comes to hearing, his clearly is selective.

He says, "You know with those ratings they're just talking about the mechanics. About the reliability. No one talks about the actual value that it brings to the toast." He says it with a hint of condescension, with just enough tone meant to make me feel a little irrational, if not gullible and stupid. He's never liked being corrected.

"Either way, I don't think the salesman expects—"

"If it doesn't toast right, then you won't use it, and therefore you won't have toast. Hearing or no hearing."

In the box store rumored to be going out of business, in the back near the washing machines, he stops and touches the tip of his index finger to my chest, leaving it there like the bell of a stethoscope. The *Consumer Reports* hangs out of his waistband. For being a middle-aged project consultant, sometimes my friend Tom can be a real gunslinger.

He says, "Time to ride out of Dodge. No point in wasting time on something that will just let you down."

Over the next several months, my friend Tom works to contradict the odds. He's calculated the ratio of each passing year to the reduction of our friend pool, with the conclusion that the probability for his eventual demise is only increasing. And that, he says, is a trend he's determined to reverse. He dedicates weeks to weightlifting at the gym, something entirely new to him, charting the relationship between increased muscle mass and white blood cell production. While there is no question that the exercise is positive for the body, he cannot quite make the conclusive determination that it actually is improving his odds in the way he hoped—at least not enough to counteract the intense boredom of being at the gym and the distaste he has in himself for his predilection towards competing with anyone who is within eyeshot. So, then my friend Tom focuses his attention to his diet, determining the exact proportions of high carb and high fat that he presumes primitive man ate, which in turn led primitive man to evolve. It should make sense.

My friend Tom was thrice married. He used to lament his lousy luck for finding the wrong woman three times in a row. Only lately has he been looking inward.

Tom denies that he said what he said about being a Nervous Christian type. He says he couldn't have said it because he's never believed in God. Maybe, he suggests, he was talking in general or metaphorical terms, and I might have heard it wrong or conflated it with some other conversation or book or article.

Why argue?

I ask if he's sleeping better these nights.

He says, "Except for when they appear in my dreams."

I ask what he means, and he tells me that Vanessa was walking around in his head last night, and it gave him no comfort.

"Some people say the opposite."

"Some people are willing to believe anything."

I'm reminded of a confession he made years ago about a terrifying evening in the Hollywood Hills in the late sixties, one in which he and his girlfriend had been attacked during a botched dope deal. In the mayhem he'd seen what I took to be the infamous Paul McCartney head hidden in the sage brush, although it was something he would not name, only saying it was a vision that stuck with him, popping up at random times ever since. When he told me, he described it as *mysterious* and *haunted*. It's funny to imagine such abstract words coming from someone who, as he's aged, has come to strive for the reliability of indubitable certainties.

My friend Tom continues to press his case, saying, "Who wants to see ghosts walking around in your head? Who wants the eternal reminders? And why should someone who I hadn't seen in decades suddenly get a starring role? It brings me no comfort. It only calls for vigilance against the interminable."

I ask if he's taking something. A pill, over-the-counter, just to get a little sleep.

Tom says he read those only let you simulate sleep, and he doesn't want to simulate anything. At this point he's shooting for real—from everything. Instead, he says, he's been attacking the sleep issue through a new diet, and though he says he knows it sounds predictable, he is seeing if cutting out gluten will help, which leads him to ask if he told me he finally bought a toaster.

"Just in time," I say.

Anticipating that this gluten-free experiment won't last, my friend Tom says he already bought a loaf of sesame wheat bread from Gjusta, wrapped it in plastic, and put it in the freezer. After that he set up the toaster in the nearest corner of the kitchen counter, sharing the same outlet as the coffeemaker. He even threw away the box, so convinced that he'll be using the appliance before long.

He says I should come over and see it. He explains that when you sit at his breakfast table, you can see yourself reflected in its glossy steel side, slightly elongated, your expression distorted.

I remind him not to plug it in, telling him that even if it is off, a plugged-in appliance can still drain energy. I tell him they call it vampire power.

ii.

AT A table in the Pine Cove, Vanessa stopped mid-sentence, again asking where the new drummer was. Already it was December of 1980, and they were really, truly living in the future, and she didn't want to have to wait for the following one before he showed. Met with a shrug, she continued to talk about her vision for creating a punk reaction to Fleetwood Mac, and she didn't mean that bluesy sixties version of them, but rather the dreamier current Fleetwood Mac that everyone was swooning over. It bored her guts to mush. And it offended her sensibilities. Still, she wasn't *just* forming a band. Vanessa was planning a motherfucking reaction that would pound people's emotions into submission. Make them think and feel something about the world—not all those sappy kinds of lyrics.

"Of course," Vanessa said, "it's really about making an action to get a reaction. Nothing but basic physics. Action: reaction. Action: reaction." She paused. "Am I putting you to sleep?"

Layered on the second floor above a liquor store and a barbershop, the Pine Cove was packed with college students, workers from the almond factory up the street, and then people like Chick, people who liked a large dark space that felt alive and active, yet private. You hardly could see from one table to the next. Nor hear much beyond the immediate conversation and the drone of a drumbeat from a vaguely recognizable song on the jukebox.

Chick apologized, saying it had been a long day. But he assured her he was listening. The truth about Vanessa was that you didn't want to miss a word. She'd experienced a world Chick and his friends only dreamed about—L.A. in the sixties, lost weekends in Haight-Ashbury, a summer in London when she'd met the Beatles. Chick's friend Curtis was also pretty sure she'd been in New York for a spell, a Factory Girl in Andy Warhol's inner circle. Once you were in her world, it was hard to step out. The stories were just too good. Chick especially liked the one about the friend of hers who had been involved in various L.A. underworlds, only to give up the life for a more peaceful existence as a line cook on Sunset. Vanessa characterized this move as a tragedy, not just because this friend had been one of her more reliable dealers, but because the decision to step away from his former life had been the very thing that led to his murder. The moral of her story, and what stuck with Chick most of all, was that you could live your life with so much caution that it would kill you.

As long as you were buying the drinks, Vanessa would talk all night about everything and anything on her mind. Anything except for why she showed up out of the blue in sleepy Sacramento without knowing a soul and how she'd recruited people half her age to be part of her vision.

"Buy me another pitcher," she said to Chick. "And tell me again, where is this phantom drummer? None of this will work without a mean, mean drummer."

"I know," Chick said. "I know. It's like the third time you've asked tonight about when he's showing up."

"To quote Auric Goldfinger, 'Once is happenstance. Twice is coincidence. Three times is enemy action.'"

The first try at a drummer hadn't lasted a night. It only had taken him ten minutes to figure out that Vanessa didn't know how to play bass. In an auto repair shop that she'd arranged to use as a practice space, they stood encircled by space heaters that didn't add much warmth but instead only served to activate the pungent aroma of motor oil and grease. They'd just been running through a jam when the drummer stopped mid-beat, trying not to show his frustration at how off her playing was. Because he was a friend of Chick's, the drummer suggested that Vanessa just handle vocals. He offered to call a bassist from his old high school jazz band who could really play. Then they might be able to make something happen here.

She faced him, her bass, a sunburst Rickenbacker hanging low at her thigh, with the neck pointed up so she could reach the bottom frets. Earlier, Chick had shown her the notes to hit, mirroring them slowly on his guitar as she followed along. But it was a different story once they'd begun playing, when her fingers stumbled up and down the fretboard, landing with no particular pattern.

She told the drummer, "We're not the high school jazz orchestra." The band would sound right when the feeling and attitude was right. "It's never about *notes*."

As they downed the new pitcher, Vanessa told Chick this supposed new drummer better be caveman primal. There could be no technicians in her band. Those types only knew how to follow instructions. Like snapping together precut puzzle pieces.

"This," she declared, "is a time for madness."

A small cheer rose from the bar, where, in the corner, the TV played the Monday Night Football game.

Vanessa said, "Why don't you call him?"

"Call him?"

"Who have we been talking about? The drummer. Phone the drummer and see if he forgot."

"He's a good guy."

"Whatever. The planet is full of good guys. But we're the ones losing time. We're sitting around just absorbing the world when we should be pushing back against it." She pointed to the group of mostly men huddled in front of the football game. "Just look at them," she said. "Do I need to say anything more?"

Chick scooted his chair back and stood. He reached into his pocket for a dime.

Tall and thin, Vanessa always was uniformed in black jeans and a
white T-shirt under a black sweatshirt. Her dyed red hair, cut at
an angle, emphasized her high cheek bones. Sneakily imposing,
Vanessa was a high-pressure system whose presence immediately
shifted and reshaped the energy in any space she entered. She
eschewed anything tied to tradition, something she titled *compla-
cency*. Being left behind with the status quo was the most terrifying place to be in Vanessa's world. And she wanted everyone to
share that fear. Her go-to example was her special disdain for
people's reverence for The Beatles. Tired. Overplayed. Nothing
more than idolatry. She called the near constant recycling of the
group's mythology a form of corporate mind control. Sometimes
it rang as personal. Maybe from her younger days in London. At
just the mention of them, almost as a reflex, Vanessa would snarl
and enunciate the line from the Clash: "*phony Beatlemania has bitten
the dust.*"

Vanessa was the type of person you rarely saw in this town. To
Chick, it was intoxicating.

After the seventh ring, Chick hung up the payphone. It was down
a corridor, just outside the bathroom, and he wanted to get away
from the stink seeping out under the door. He'd done his part. It
was a stupid exercise but one that would placate Vanessa. The
drummer surely was on the way by now. He'd told Chick he was
totally into Vanessa's idea and promised he'd be there. Once
Chick could get back to the table, he'd remind Vanessa it wasn't
even nine o'clock yet. People don't just appear the moment you
conjure them.

Coming back down the hall, he heard the bartender yell for
everyone to be quiet, followed by a wave of shushes cascad-
ing through the house. The barback, a woman named Barb
who Chick knew from the clubs, was standing on a milk crate,
stretched and turning up the volume of the football game. With
her other hand, she tugged down on the hem of her thermal
shirt riding up the small of her back. She had the balance of an
Olympian.

From the television set, Howard Cosell had just announced that John Lennon was dead. Spoken somberly and without doubt, Cosell already was eulogizing, clearly working to maintain his composure, unable to hold on to any illusion that the sport he was covering actually mattered or had purpose.

The Pine Cove never had been so quiet. For a moment, Chick couldn't remember the route to his table.

Barb flipped the channels. Lennon's face was on every screen.

When Chick found his way back, Vanessa was gone. Her glass sat in front of her chair, partially full, fresh foam bubbling on the rim. A wrinkled napkin sat beside it. On it, she'd written "*Drummer??*"

Could she really have left between the time he was on the phone and when he returned to the table?

The room remained stunned in silence. Immobile. Hardly anyone even raised a glass as they strained to listen to the news reports from New York that John Lennon had been shot outside his apartment building, cutting to tributes and static cameras of people gathering outside his home. Before long, you could feel everyone in the bar getting restless, too wound up to sit still. A young guy stumbled back from the payphone and reported that KZAP was holding an impromptu candlelight vigil in Gallo Park. One by one, people stood and slid on their coats, a silent line of mourners heading over to the vigil, only the TV news as a soundtrack.

Chick decided he needed to wait, figuring Vanessa would be back. Plus, he had a duty to wait for the drummer. He'd promised.

He waited until it was only him, the staff, and three almond workers at the bar who demanded the game come on already.

At ten o'clock, Chick scooted his chair back. Vanessa's half-drunken beer still sat on the table. He downed it in one gulp and swore that he could taste her breath on the rim.

At Gallo Park, Chick looked for her among the burning white candles. Despite her regular dismissal of The Beatles, maybe Vanessa had been driven to grief and pity by this news. This was no night to be alone. He thought he saw her across the park. But when he pushed his way over toward the I Street side, past the empty fountain, he didn't see her. He didn't see anyone who even looked like her. Chick did spot the drummer. By then, he knew it didn't matter.

Over the next few days and weeks he watched for Vanessa every time he went out. After a month, his vigilance dwindled. By then he'd lost the image of her in his mind. Forgot the feeling of her presence. If he had to be honest about it, Chick wasn't even sure he knew who he was looking for anymore.

iii.

Paul McCartney Interviews Himself (April 17, 1970)

Q: Are you planning a new album or single with the Beatles?

PAUL: No.

Q: Is this album a rest away from the Beatles or the start of a solo career?

PAUL: Time will tell. Being a solo album means it's "the start of a solo career. . ." and not being done with the Beatles means it's just a rest. So it's both.

Q: Is your break with the Beatles temporary or permanent, due to personal differences or musical ones?

PAUL: Personal differences, business differences, musical differences, but most of all because I have a better time with my family. Temporary or permanent? I don't really know.

Q: Do you foresee a time when Lennon-McCartney becomes an active songwriting partnership again?

PAUL: No.

iv.

A COP stopped traffic for the photographer. The photographer fumbled with his lens while he stepped backward over the zebra intersection toward his stepladder in the middle of the road. Moments later, the Beatles, all four of them, so rarely seen together anymore, came out from behind the tall blond doors of Abbey Road studios and descended down the stoop. They waited on the pavement, adjusting each other's collars, dabbing the sweat off their foreheads. Finally, the photographer climbed the rungs and signaled he was ready. The four of them walked back and forth across the crosswalk several times. The cop did his best to hold people back. After snapping six pictures, the photographer raised his hand. He'd gotten what he needed.

She only caught the last few minutes or so of the shoot. Barely getting there in time and fighting for breath as she tried to get closer, she was stopped up the block by the policeman.

Vanessa claims she did end up in the background of one of the outtakes. A fan magazine ran some of them. Despite pointing herself out, no one can ever really see her. But she's there. It's a blur. A smudge of red under a tree in the far distance. She insists. Whatever.

With the window open and the curtains blowing, from her motel room you can see the edge of the Abbey Road billboard. Everyone's been talking about the sign. And there it is, just below us, Vanessa, me, and the woman who would become my wife. Vanessa has just returned after living abroad, a time during which, reportedly, she met the Beatles. We were just supposed to meet her in the lobby and then go down to the beach to meet some of her friends. But now we're sitting on the edge of the bed while Vanessa fiddles with her eyeliner in the bathroom.

I ask, "I take it Paul still had his head when you got to Abbey Road?"

The breeze is cold through the open window, and so I pull over one of the pillows and lay it across my lap. The woman who

would become my wife glances at me, squinting and shaking her
head in disapproval. It could be the joke is too insensitive. Or
maybe it's that the pillow is too intimate.

She doesn't like to talk about it, Vanessa. It seems she's not
keen on mistakes. Even less so on accountability.

"If only," she says.

"What? Why do you say that?"

Vanessa drops her lash curler; it tings against the sink and then
bounces under the toilet. Bending over to get it, she says, "He's
no John or George."

"Nor Ringo," I add.

Standing back up, she says, "Let's not take this too far."

Here's all I know: Vanessa was more than a bystander. She was an
Apple Scruff. George came up with the moniker. He later wrote a
song about them. The Beatles knew the Scruffs by name. When
they'd come to meetings at Apple Corps on Savile Row or head
uptown to the studio to record, each band member made sure to
say hello to the loyal Scruffs waiting to greet them. Some of the
boys were more engaging than the others. John once stopped and
thanked Vanessa for being among those who had helped to pack
the record he'd made with Yoko, a last-minute process that had
had to be undertaken in-house after the distributor balked at the
couple standing naked on an album cover. He looked her in the
eye. Yoko touched her shoulder. You could sense an allegiance
to John.

There's a trace of an accent in Vanessa, but it doesn't sound
faked, instead like something one picks up by being around too
many people who talk the same. Her demeanor, well, that is an
affect. For being a Southern Californian, there is a Britishness
about her. Earlier, when we were introduced, I told her that, or
something along those lines. Sometimes you have no clue that
you're saying the very things someone wants to hear.

Vanessa strolls out of the bathroom like she's taking the stage and heads straight for the window. She pulls shut the curtain. She says she doesn't want to see it anymore, the billboard. She says she never liked him much anyway.

I ask, "Paul?"

"Who else?" And she says the week before the album cover shoot, he'd arrived alone at the studio and stopped to say hi to all the regular Scruffs. Even though she stood among them, smiling and nodding right there in front of him, doing her best to engage, he didn't acknowledge her. Later, an Apple Scruff, trying to be helpful and sincere, told her that there had been so many others like her who came and went. "'You can tell right away. This is a life, not an activity. The boys understand that. They recognize who is who. Nothing personal, but it's just the way it is.'"

Vanessa says, "I wanted to say: 'What about that John thanked me? And Yoko touched my shoulder?' But you know what . . . whatever."

My first thought is that maybe she's the one who stole the head.

The afternoon in the motel was the last time the three of us were ever alone together. She told the woman who would become my wife that I reminded her too much of too much.

I said, "You need to explain."

The woman who would become my wife said, "I thought I just did."

Nearly forty years later, at age ninety-six, Paul Cole died. He was Vanessa's nemesis, a retired American businessman on vacation who found himself wandering down Abbey Road on the afternoon of the photo session. In a new sports coat and horn-rimmed glasses, he struck up a conversation with some policemen in a black van and inadvertently ended up on the album cover, just over John's left shoulder. That afternoon on Abbey Road had meant nothing to him at the time. He described looking over at the Beatles and just thinking they were a "bunch of kooks . . . radicals." He didn't even remember the whole incident until some time later, when he saw the album cover. His wife had bought it because she'd taken a liking to the song "Something."

"So obscenely unfair," Vanessa had said. Who could argue?

Reading Paul Cole's obituary made me more than a little sad for Vanessa, thinking about how all of us who knew her had humored her about the red smudge in the outtake. And it drove me to the computer to find the photos, to look hard for the smudge of red under a tree in the far distance. And, truth be told, I couldn't even remember which was the photo she'd insisted upon. But even after looking at all six, I found no smudge or indication of anything even close. So what.

People like Paul Cole. The Apple Scruffs. People like Paul McCartney.

Whatever.

John thanked her. Yoko touched her.

v.

It ENDS with a series of late-night social media posts, starting with when Vanessa begged for someone to call 911 immediately. She said her cell phone was destroyed. And then she followed up with a posting that showed a picture of her bed—perfectly made with beautiful white linens, but with splatters of blood visible on the pillows. You can see a bass in the far corner. The next post, time stamped within the half hour, said she was on her way to jail. It was written in the third person. Below that last post, under the guise of compassion, someone had commented with a scathing critique of Vanessa and her behaviors. "*You need to stop doing this. How old are you now?*" One didn't need to know her to feel how much it hurt.

There was a moment when Chick could've jumped into this dialogue and defended her against this bully, but he hesitated, not sure if it was his place to get involved. By morning all three posts had disappeared.

It is one of his great moments of shame, that hesitation.

When she died, his first thought was how his burden could never be lifted. It was something he was going to have to live with forever. That alone made him feel even worse. He was still looking for her in the candlelit park.

The Legend Hosts a Screening

i.

IT'S A curious situation. He is by all definitions a Hollywood movie legend. For over twenty years, he's acted in movies that defined the art form as a cornerstone of popular culture. Even people who don't know his movies know him. He's become an icon. A symbol of glamorous Hollywood. And though his name is as solidly American as the ground itself, in fact he was born with a Polish surname, barely pronounceable to the American tongue. Raised in New York tenements, he knew nothing of the razzle-dazzle upbringing later afforded to his children. But it would be unfair to him to say he never could have imagined it, this life. In fact, as a boy and as a young man, he persevered through pure drive, a self-determined passion for books and later for theater—all fuel for the engine of his ambition.

In his Beverly Hills mansion on Canon Drive, where the evening sunset turns the beige stucco and brick red Spanish tiled roof into a single rose color, the legend finds himself as far from those beginnings as possible. But at heart he remains a fighter, still battling against a class system that once convinced his parents that the bottom of the heap was as high as they could ever get. Even at the height of his fame, he notably fought Joe McCarthy and the blacklists. He refused to name a soul. Hired writers and crew members who were told they'd never work again. He'd been a staunch supporter of the unions and a champion advocate for putting an end to the unfair studio system.

So then why is he so militantly offended by his actor son's generation? Why does he refer to them with words like *naïve* and *dreamy* and *irrelevant?* He is no supporter of Nixon. No proponent of the war in Vietnam. And yet even this celebrated actor can't mask the rancor he feels towards his children's generation. Baffled by their informality, baffled by their lack of respect for what came before them, he withdraws, sometimes ashamed.

His only salvation is the belief that eventually they'll grow up, see, and appreciate that a world can be left to them not just by the likes of Richard Nixon and Barry Goldwater and Ronald Reagan, but also by people like him, who also have worked to make it a little better. But for now, it's a conversation that can't be had. It only would become an argument, one he concedes would be useless until they one day reach his age.

ii.

A SMALL constellation of guests crowds the living room, awaiting the screening of *Paint Your Wagon* that will be previewed in the legend's home theater. Although not excessively large in its architectural footprint, thanks to the mathematical eye of an interior designer with a keen sense of space, his living room feels twice its size. Festive and intimate, tonight is a reminder of an industry that enshrines its icons, keeping them young and beautiful in perpetuity.

The legend moves with precision, small shifts and turns, pirouettes. Under his cashmere turtleneck sweater, his broad shoulders grow more heroic with each step. Person to person, he greets each guest. He hasn't stopped talking. No one should feel unwelcome. And it looks so natural, his choreography. It would be nearly impossible for any observer to note that each glissade and chassé is but footwork that allows him to keep his back to the far corner of the room, thus avoiding eye contact with his son and the conversation he doesn't wish to have.

Near the sliding glass door, his son stands with his girlfriend and her young boy. He's dressed in his regular uniform: a brown corduroy sport coat and blue jeans. His son wears it on talk shows, to interviews. It's his *look*. He claims the jacket offers him his own identity—an essential distinction because, in addition to a name and vocation, he and his father also share facial features and natural expressions.

Sometimes his son doesn't think about what he says.

The legend is afraid of being drawn into a situation with his son in which he'll find himself reacting, rebuking him for how he dressed on a night when he knew his father prepared introductions with colleagues who could help bring the book everyone seems to love to the screen. It's embarrassing. Did his son already forget that he went out on a limb for him? Called in favors? There still is an expectation of protocol and decorum in this business. Including the way you dress. But the legend sidesteps the confrontation. It's best. Slipping into the superficial will only subvert and obscure the deeper issue that stabs at him: the idea that a son can be so dedicated to distancing himself from his father.

It cannot be avoided. The legend's son loops his arm around his father in greeting as the boy and his mother step back.

On cue a woman joins their half-circle, pinching a cracker and cheddar cheese between her thumb and forefinger. Knowing she'd likely take a financial interest in his son's film project, the legend also believes she could ward off his son's more radical and experimental inclinations, instead keeping him rooted in cinematic tradition. Her hair is fixed. Skin polished and lacquered. Every detail, from the lines in her face to the vase of her neck to each hair of her narrowly arched eyebrows, looks artful and unique in its sublimity.

She greets the actor with a kiss to the cheek, saying, "I was just asking your father if you'd be here. And now, it seems, with a family, even."

From the other side of the glass door, lights ripple off the swimming pool, casting gems across all their faces.

The legend takes a step back while the actor introduces his girlfriend. Before his eyes, his son's mannerisms change. Hand gestures become more deliberate and precise, the edges of each of word clipped and sculpted in near perfect elocution. The actor has just walked onstage.

They are father and son.

Somewhat theatrically, the woman turns toward the boy, raising up the cheese and cracker, and taps her index finger to her ear. A pearl earring catches the light. She says, "I don't know that I heard this one's name. And who is our little Beatle?"

Black-vested caterers balance silver trays weighed down by a variety of toothpicked salmon and beef filets, little sandwiches, and glasses of wine.

The woman tells the boy her name, noting she's sure that means nothing to him, which she claims is refreshing, saying that other than the actor, and him only because of his father, no one under thirty would know half the people gathered under this roof. She adds, "But, at least for now, thankfully we still have some power and clout to guide what comes out of Hollywood. Otherwise, just imagine."

"Ten minutes," the legend announces, turning to the rest of the room. "The movie will be starting in the rec room outside. . . . Ten more minutes to eat and drink me out of house and home." To his son and the woman he adds, "You two should finish up this conversation later. I think you both will have a lot to talk about."

Patting the top of the boy's head, the woman says, "Nice to meet you, little Beatle." When she steps past him, the boy brushes at his hair. First, some crumbs. Then a piece of orange cheese that falls to the floor.

The legend always is in full control, a conductor in this world waving the baton and keeping time. He sees himself as someone who people should always have faith in, whose harshest critics consistently have gotten his sense of character wrong.

When he sent out the invitation to the evening's preview, his son asked why he'd picked an old-fashioned, classic musical with a lot of Broadway songs and a romance storyline. There were so many others that spoke to the day: *Butch Cassidy and the Sundance*

Kid, Midnight Cowboy, Z, Easy Rider, Alice's Restaurant, or even *The Arrangement.*

Why not meet the times?

But clearly his son missed the point. Tonight's showing is not a stubborn statement or a way to deny the volume of contemporary voices. Instead, it's for the legend and his generation to feel solidarity in the idea that despite what is being reported in the public sphere, the world is not spinning out of control. It's as charming and mannered as it ever has been.

iii.

SQUATTING, the legend lowers himself until he and the boy are at the same level, eye to eye. "You must be bored beyond belief." The party orbits above them. You could reach up and touch it. He tells the boy he looks like he's all alone in this room full of people.

The boy glances up at his mom, unsure of what to say, unsure of the line between polite and rude and where any reply might fall.

"Sure you are," the legend says. "How could you not be?"

He nods in agreement, the boy. It is true.

"Come with me. I want to show you something."

As they walk across the living room, the two of them holding hands, the boy ingests the power of the legend, feeling the space parting, as though the room reshapes itself, shaking out and elongating its dimensions.

Standing outside in the backyard, the legend points to a replica of the ancient Grecian statue, *The Winged Victory of Samothrace.* Lit up by footlights, the figure rests sequestered in her own space on the terrace.

The party continues behind the sliding glass door. Muted, everyone's hand gestures and facial expressions look silly and exaggerated.

This, the legend says, is what he wanted to show the boy. "You'll never feel bored when you look at her."

Armless, her body is slightly arched back, wings revved up in flight. Reflections of the emerald light off the pool make this goddess Nike suggest she is in motion, gliding in a graceful descent.

It takes a moment for the boy to realize she is headless. The base of her neck, broken and rough-edged.

The legend kneels down, looking up from the same vantage point as the boy. "Isn't she beautiful," he says. "Powerful." He tells the boy to close his eyes and imagine Nike landing out of the sky, one hand raised and the other cupped around her mouth as she declares victory over a battle.

The boy lowers his eyelids. He trusts the legend.

"Can you see it. . . ? Are you imagining it?"

"Kind of."

"Only kind of?"

Peeking for a moment, the boy sees the legend also has his eyes closed. "What happened to her head?" he whispers, as though Nike might hear and feel ashamed.

"Lost, I imagine. Knocked over. Left and forgotten. It's common with a lot of ancient statues."

"I wonder where they go. All those heads."

"I'll tell you something: When I look at her, I don't even notice. I always see her head. Her face. Her expression. She's telling me that every obstacle, the things that stand in your way, are only problems right now. She reminds me of the power of civilization, of being civilized, and how we're all in a timeless history together. . . . Now, squeeze your eyes even tighter. Tight, tight, tight. Look at her. Look and look and look. Can you see her now? Her face?"

The boy pinches his face and clenches his teeth with all of his might, trying to tighten up his brain and force a picture of her face to appear on it. But all he gets is the moment on Sunset Boulevard when Paul McCartney's head dashed off into the Hollywood Hills. Maybe that is where the all heads go, he considers.

The boy sneaks a peak again. The legend's eyes remain closed. His lips move ever so slightly, as if in a dream. Before the boy shuts his eyes again, willing to try to join the legend in this dream world, he reaches over and takes the legend's hand. It is secure. It is welcoming.

In the Canyon

i.

DURBIN SAID that of course it was a political act. Everything we do, he said, is both an act and inherently political. It stands to reason.

He was someone the woman who would become my wife sort of knew, with an emphasis on *sort of*, because she'd never been able to tell me if Durbin was his first name, last name, or even a nickname, always backing out of that conversation by declaring, "What does it matter."

Several of us sat on a living room floor in Silver Lake, and I was petting the soft strands of an alpaca rug that one of Durbin's roommates had hauled across Nepal on his back. Or so he said. This was not a place I really wanted to be. This group had been friends before the woman who would become my wife and I had met, and they always were looking at me as though I didn't measure up to her. Lately, it was something I'd also been suspecting.

Durbin was talking about the murder of Sharon Tate and of the music teacher in the canyon (as was everyone in town), but to make his point that everything was subject to his theory, he broadened his scope to include the recent Haymarket bombing by the Weather Underground, the latest murders of the Zodiac Killer, and even last month's desecrated Abbey Road sign.

The last one was something I knew about, having seen it more than once. The others I'd been willfully ignoring, hearing only enough details to know that I couldn't bear to hear any more. I said I thought that the billboard issue was more about vandalism than politics.

"They are not exclusive. One is the natural outcome of the other." He spoke as though constructing a proof, pausing as if he were selecting just the precise word. "The message of the vandal is a statement against the body politic, and thus, any destruction is, in turn, a de facto curse on the dominant societal structure."

The others nodded along, as though his ability to respond so quickly was evidence of his intellectual superiority.

He could barely meet my eyes. It was stupid, Durbin's logic. Any one of the dozen thoughts I was having would have exposed him as a fraud. Ideas like Durbin's always wilted once they were exposed to daylight.

The woman who would become my wife cut off this part of the conversation.

"Okay," she said. "That's enough from both of you."

If I didn't know better, I would have thought that she was trying to spare me humiliation. Or worse, she was afraid that I would somehow embarrass her.

The whole thing was hard to stomach. This was the kind of situation that was really unhealthy for us.

I'd thought a lot about that guy, Monty. And even more so what his co-worker at the diner had said when he'd dropped the news of Monty's death—how the sign's mutilation had caused a curse over the valley. To be honest, at the time I bought into it. Sometimes you need something to make you feel that there's some logic to it all. Then I got to thinking: What if the vandalized Paul McCartney head wasn't the curse, but instead the byproduct of a larger curse? I mean, just pick up a random newspaper from the past two years. What better logic was there?

She begged me not to make a joke about it. "Please," she said. "Please, please, please." She didn't have to worry. There was no way on earth I could think of one.

A field agent from the FBI had just left. He'd come to tell me that investigators had found my father's name on what they believed to be a Manson Family hit list. The register of names was long, he'd said. Too long to be carried out in any reasonable manner. That was supposed to make it a little better.

"*My* father?" I'd recited as a refrain each time he finished a sentence. The field agent suspected it must have stemmed from some interaction that had taken place a while ago.

I'd said, "You mean because it's been seven years since he got sick?"

We stayed up most of the night in bed talking about it, she and I. It could've been anything, I said. He'd been a doctor. Maybe one of those followers had been a disgruntled patient. Or an unhappy worker at the hospital.

She asked if the reason really was the issue.

Hoping to soothe her, I said to remember that my father already was dead, something that still killed me to say aloud.

We turned on the bedroom television to keep our minds from jumping at every little sound. And then we turned it down because we thought we should keep alert to every little sound.

By 2:00 a.m. she'd fallen asleep. All of the TV networks had signed off for the night.

I tucked her in as tightly and securely as I could, and then leaned back against the headboard, trying to close my eyes. But it was hard when the electrical crackles and pops of the TV sounded like voices or other things coming from down the hall.

It was impossible to know what was what.

Even when I was certain I heard footsteps, there was no temptation to call the police. Perhaps it was an innate understanding of the relationship between fear, paranoia, and imagination. Or maybe just embarrassment. Picturing it from the perspective of the field agent, he believed that having the information prevented harm, not predicted it. In fact, when he'd been here, you could sense the agent's frustration that we were not taking this news with relief.

And still, all I could think about was the woman who would become my wife. As she slept, her breaths came in short bursts. This was no time to take any chances.

Stealthily, I slid out of bed and tiptoed down the hall, surveying all directions before every step. A few of the paintings on the walls were slightly tilted. Everything was so quiet. For just a moment I felt like the only one left in the world, wandering through it, almost sad to be alive.

Once inside the kitchen, I snatched a butcher knife out of the block and scampered over to double check the locks. In each room and then eventually coming down the hallway, I was a savage leading with his blade, the dull metal lighting up in sharp strikes of moonlight.

The thought of anything happening to her terrified me.

Under the pillow, my sweaty palm gripped the knife's handle. All I wanted was to drift off, to cut the wiring in my brain that was sending around a million possibilities and scenarios.

I tried to ingest her breath. She'd been really frightened. You could tell it was going to last a long time. Maybe even be the kind of thing that shapes us.

We never asked for it. And yet, this was the world we were delivered.

ii.

IF THE traffic is right, the actor's house, in the woods of Topanga Canyon, is only a half hour or so away from the boy's home. At the end of a long dirt road, it looks more like a vacation cabin—rustic gray boards for siding, a flat roof, and wide-open rooms—surrounded by a forest of laurel and oak and walnut trees that build and build and build up to the edge of the property line before they seemingly shoot straight down the canyon. Sitting inside it, you can think you're in the only house within a million-mile radius.

The boy is here for an overnight while his mother tries to deal with Tom and Julieta. They have flipped the script to the point that it's as though the boy and his mother are the interlopers. She says it's something better handled between adults.

Normally, the actor's place is one the boy loves to visit. There's even a girl a couple of houses down with a rope swing over the canyon where the neighborhood kids gather, and though he hasn't had the nerve to try it himself, the boy loves to watch them swing, cheering them on from a safe distance.

But that was before.

Now, staying overnight makes him a little nervous. Just two days before Charles Manson's killing spree, the actor had been dining and socializing with Sharon Tate and friends in Beverly Hills, no more than a couple of miles away from the legend's home. And now, it seems, the strange and unsettling murder of the music teacher just down the road from here also was connected to the Manson spree.

But it's not sleeping over in Topanga Canyon at this moment of time that gets to the boy. Nor is it the proximity between the actor and the murders. It's the sense that anything that happens in one place can drift up and over the city and land right in front of you.

The actor is worked up; he can't find his airline ticket. Late to-morrow afternoon, he's supposed to fly off to Berlin to meet an important director who is looking to break into the American market. It was arranged by one his father's friends. With one movie star already willing to commit, she's coached the actor that, in the eyes of the studios, convincing the German director to join in on the project for the book everyone seems to love will be the de facto green light.

But now he's panicking that he won't be able to go if he can't find the ticket.

For the past half hour, he's been tearing the house upside down, rifling through drawers, searching all of his pockets, shaking the pages of every book and magazine. Meanwhile, the boy wanders the living room, looking under the couch pillows, under the pile of mail in the kitchen, in dish cupboards and other places the ticket never would be.

Charging out of the bedroom into the living room, the actor walks straight into the kitchen and sorts through the pile of mail that he and the boy already have been through more than once. He tosses it back on the counter. Two envelopes fall on the tile floor.

Maybe it's time to call the boy's mother, he says. Request that she rummage through his belongings at her house. It's something neither wants to do. It will mean asking her to go into her bedroom where Tom and Julieta remain holed up. They still have not left the house for over a week now. Still too afraid of the outside world.

They both stand there, the actor and the boy. Feet apart, the actor's face half-lit by the sunlight shining through the crack in the curtain. Like the comedy-tragedy mask.

Both jump when there comes a knock on the door. A series of steady raps that could only belong to someone familiar.

"Can you get that?" the actor asks. "I need to go through the bedroom once more."

It is not something the boy wants to do. Given the Manson situation and the fact that part of it took place right down the street, he prefers to keep the outside world outside. At least for the time being.

Pinching the lace curtain and holding it to the side, he peeks through the window, seeing the mother of the little girl who lives at the house with the rope swing. Her feet dance in place. She again knocks on the door, a little more insistent. It rattles the lamp shade behind the couch.

"Can you please get that," the actor calls back.

The boy drops the curtain; it swings back and forth, a shivering breeze crossing his neck. Slowly, he unlatches the lock and turns the handle, ready to slam shut the door if a stranger appears behind her.

In general, the little girl's mother is friendly by nature, pleasant and gracious. Always a welcoming smile. But now, as her fingers drum against her hip, she looks past him, peering over his shoulder into the living room. Her eyes settle on the stray envelopes scattered on the kitchen floor.

"Have you two been playing?"

The boy shakes his head.

She asks, "Willow hasn't been here?"

From the bedroom, the actor asks who's there at the door.

"It's Sally," the mother says. Her voice is higher than usual. She sounds short of breath. On the edge of angry. "Have you seen Willow here?"

The actor ambles down the hallway, his hands laced behind his head, elbows winged out. His T-shirt pulls up, revealing his slim waist. It could be a magazine cover.

"I don't know," he says. To the boy he asks, "Have we?"

Sally cuts in. "He said she hasn't."

"Well there you go," the actor says. "If we do see Willow, we'll let her know you're looking for her. Or better yet, I'll send her straight home." He steps backward, trying to disengage.

Sally stands firm in the doorway. Her expression draws blank, matching her gaze. "No one has seen her all day. When I got out of bed, Willow wasn't home. She's been gone since then, or before. Not a single neighbor . . . No one has seen her."

The actor's eyes glance up at the clock. He says he's sure she'll show up. "You know kids, Sally."

They all try to forget what's on everyone's mind up here in the canyon.

Perched on the ledge of the couch, a sliver of curtain pulled back, the boy watches out the window.

Outside, the grounds are still, other than a light wind bending all the stalks and branches down toward the edge of the canyon. It is peaceful in spite of what might be lurking just below the surface.

The actor comes back from his bedroom. He stops in the kitchen to pick up the two envelopes off the floor. He looks again at them, holding them as if somehow he missed the ticket the first two times. "Okay," he says. "Which one of us is it? Who's going to call your mom?"

The boy doesn't want to move. To take his eyes off the grounds is to give up hope. "I need to watch for Willow."

"There a good chance it could be in my sport coat, in her closet. I have a vague memory."

"I can't," the boy says, and saying it makes him feel as dumb and helpless as it makes him feel worthy. For a moment, he questions if he has the wherewithal.

"Look," the actor says. He leans over and squeezes the boy's shoulders. He can read the agony. "Don't worry. Sally does this all the time. And half the time Willow's actually playing under her bed while her mother riles up the whole neighborhood."

The boy keeps watch out the window.

The actor shuffles the two letters, top to bottom, over and over.

Neither wants to make the call. Who wants to ask his mom to have to cross into her occupied bedroom? Who wants to be the one to summon the issue of Tom and Julieta? In fact, when either of them really thinks about it, who wants to be the one to summon anything that is lurking behind closed doors?

iii.

In a phone booth on West 5th Street, across from the library, Michael's hands shook. His breath steamed the glass walls. Three times in a row he dropped his dime while trying to insert it into the slot. Three times in a row the coin wedged itself in the same exact spot under the folding door, forcing him to crouch and twist around, smelling the greasy old piss stain in the corner, while he worked the dime out with his longest fingernail.

In a mere six days since he'd disappeared into the Hollywood Hills, the world had turned inside-out, to one in which hippies and freaks—the good guys—were murdering actors and teachers. No one was safe anymore. Michael didn't know what to do. Where to turn. Who to trust. And yet he had to make it work. So he hid out in public on a bench in Pershing Square. Smoked the last of the hash in his pipe. Took any pills he could score. But nothing made a difference. Music didn't make a difference. Getting stoned didn't make a difference. Cassie was the only thing he thought might make a difference. His only reliable connection to the world.

Michael danced in place while Cassie's phone rang about a hundred million times. When it picked up, he froze. His back foot perched on its toes. Her *hello* sounded mannered and rehearsed, kind of robotic. At first, he thought it was her mom.

"Hello," Cassie said again.

It was her and it wasn't her.

He couldn't bring himself to speak. Instead, Michael just listened to her breathe. He could feel the warmth crawling down his neck, comforting, like when she'd lean over him to take a hit from the pipe he was holding.

"I don't know who this is," she said, her voice rising. "But I wish you'd stop calling, and if you don't, I'm calling the police."

Stop calling? Yes, he'd thought about phoning several times. But he hadn't actually done it until now. *Stop* calling? This was the first time he'd reached out to her since returning down from the hills.

"Do you hear me, creep? I'll call the police."

It was clear: she too had been infected by the fear of the moment. It trembled along the edges and curves of every word. Spun round and round until—and who would ever imagine—heading straight for the cops had become her default.

He heard Cassie whisper to her mom or dad that no one is saying anything. Muffled, something was said back to her.

Finally, she announced in full voice, "I'm hanging up now!"

Michael dropped the phone. The receiver dangled near his knees, its braided silver cord glimmering from the streetlight. Leaning against the glass wall, he slid down to the floor, balling himself into the corner. He knew his inner strength was on reserve. Running on fumes. Already he knew he risked slipping away.

Reaching up, Michael grabbed the swaying phone and hugged it against his cheek, trying to find the last bit of Cassie's warm breath.

Michael stayed curled in the phone booth until sunrise, singing "Blackbird" to himself, trying to keep from completely crawling into his own empty chest.

 When the door shut quickly after him, all heads turned, certain
that either this was a protester about to make a scene or another
downtown druggie who was lost. The décor of the Armed Forces
Induction Center on South Broadway looked mobile and provi-
sional. An old storefront, hollow and long. Desks. Phones. Posters
on the wall. Clipboard and pens. A space appointed merely by
where its supplies had happened to land.
    Michael slumped into a folding chair near the front window,
his legs crossed tightly while his hands rubbed and scratched
at his neck. He was tired. Sore and wrecked after spending a
cramped night in the phone booth. His shoulders were damp
from the light rain he'd walked through, hair stringy and plastered against his neck. Not even sure how he got here—only
that it was as if he'd been guided—Michael looked out at the
street, still determined, counting raindrops that purled down
the window.
    He waited nearly forty minutes while the recruiters took their
time with other boys as though testing whether he would see this
through.
    Across the room, hanging on the wall, a framed recruiting ad-
vertisement read "MAN'S WORK" in big bold letters. Its accompanying image showed a line of four soldiers crossing a murky river.
The point man approached tall shoreline grasses with his rifle
readied, trailed by one soldier holding his weapon high above his
head and another with his finger cusped on the trigger, aiming
at something beyond the frame. But it was the third in line who
caught Michael's attention. With no visible weapon, he waded
nearly shoulder-deep in the river, lightly staring off into his own
world.
    The poster didn't mention shitty politics. Lies built upon lies.
Risk and suffering. Fear and moral uncertainty. Only the slogan:
"MAN'S WORK."

Finally, from the near corner of the room, a recruiter pointed a ballpoint pen at him. "How can we help you?" he asked, rolling his shoulders back to counter his adolescent's slouch. In real time, this sergeant's boyish face was transforming into the hardened features of a man weighted by bureaucracy.

Michael untangled himself and stood up. For a moment he felt himself continuing to rise as though lifting fully off his feet.

"I'm here," he announced.

"Yes, friend, we can see that." It was easy to imagine the sergeant as a civilian, prowling suburban streets in a cluster of indistinguishable boys, hands in his pockets, defiantly bored, hating lost freaks like Michael.

"I'm here," he said again, the words rolling out of his mouth, distant and unfamiliar. "I'm here."

"And what can we do for you now that you're here?"

"To do what you do. Take me in. Conscript me. Enlist me. I've come to sign up. I'm here."

"Well, come take a seat, friend," the sergeant said, flashing a glance at his staff sergeant.

At the desk, the sergeant explained if Michael were serious, there would be a long list of questions to get things started. Forms to fill out. Personal details, like education, criminal records, family contacts, and such. And, so everyone was duly informed, they'd also be looking at physical and mental screenings. The army needed to consider all qualifying and potentially disqualifying factors.

"But before we even begin to proceed," he said, leaning back in his chair, "maybe you can tell me why exactly why you want to enlist. Besides just being *here*, what else do you expect will happen? Did you have some specific thoughts?"

Michael might have walked out then and there. Might have walked out when the sergeant's otherwise staid demeanor cracked with an air of disdain, a little smirk that wrapped Michael in a bear hug and pressed him to say "uncle." It was like this guy *wanted* him to leave. As if he saw right through Michael. But Michael was locked into what he needed to do. He knew what was waiting for him out there in the wilds of the greater Los Angeles area. An upside-down world.

Michael held his ground. This was no time for thinking.

Not more than ten minutes after he raised his hand and swore his oath at the Armed Forces Induction Center downtown on South Broadway, Michael was sitting in the middle of a bus rolling along city streets toward the Santa Monica Freeway onramp.

Bound for Fort Ord. For basic training.

With each bump of the road, the hard seat dug deeper into his butt.

He could hardly look at the other recruits. Inner city kids. Lunks from the suburbs. Cautious warriors. Kind children dissolving into themselves. It was a part of the human race he'd never known. No one talked. They barely breathed. Lips half-parted to let the air flow in.

Doubt began to hit at him, its bundle of fists pummeling him from inside. It twisted his guts and twined his nerves.

He'd really done it this time. The ultimate stupid consequence of his irrational impulses.

At a stoplight on West 17th, just before the onramp to the Santa Monica Freeway, Michael glanced out the window, past the lump beside him who gazed emptily at the floor.

The bus rumbled in place, creaking, still trying to warm its engine since leaving the Induction Center. The sky was bright blue with only a few weak clouds. Yet it smelled of rain.

Across the street stood a liquor store, a concrete front with its name scripted in weathered red paint. Sitting in front, in folding chairs, was a line of men, all Black, all old, and all falling into each other as they laughed. One leaned forward and slapped the concrete. Another turned and spit some chew, nodding. Then they turned serious. Covering their mouths and coughing. Together, they looked up at the bus, at the collection of recruits, and these men, this lineup of old men, they shook their heads. Mournful. That really got to Michael. Mournful. Because although he might be someone who's pitied himself, he'd never perceived himself as the object of someone else's pity.

Regret started setting in. And then fear, and then shame.

As the bus continued to idle at the stoplight, the pressure began to build, radiating and percolating through his every muscle and cell—the same sense of possession that had overtaken him while playing the role of the Paul McCartney head.

Inching closer to the window for fresh air, Michael tried to ward off the familiar impulses that had driven him into the hills for days. The same ones that had led him straight to the Induction Center. He dabbed at the sweat beading on his forehead. Grabbed at his collar to loosen it, as though he might even have to tear off his shirt just to breathe. The chant from earlier in the week began to run through his head: *Rejoice the head of Paul McCartney. Rejoice.* It helped to relax his breathing. Slow his mind. *Rejoice the head of Paul McCartney. Rejoice.*

But it was impossible to find calm when he knew he'd made such a terrible mistake.

Looking up and down the aisles, Michael determined he had time to remedy his error. A few rows ahead were a couple of open windows he could squeeze through. Or, if he were sudden and deliberate enough, he could be down the aisle and out the rear emergency door, hightailing it up West 17th before anyone would know what to do.

Rejoice the head of Paul McCartney. Rejoice.

He needed to stop the loop, tamp down the impulse. Grabbing both thighs, Michael clenched a handful of skin in each hand, twisting until the pain became unbearable. For once, he needed to think something out before just acting. Slow down. Be measured. Anticipate. Consider. Don't dig the mess any deeper, especially now that you are government property.

While he debated the possibilities and potential consequences of bailing, the light changed green, and the bus began to sputter up to the onramp, axles squealing from below. Once on the ramp, the bus picked up speed, signaled, and then drifted over into the middle lane of the freeway. The guys in front of him wrestled their windows down. Michael let go of each handful of skin. The wrinkled indentations on both legs of his jeans were identical. It was frightening how quickly the burning stopped. Decades later, in an unusually lucid moment, Michael would lament to the social worker at the VA that that was the one time in his whole erratic life when he truly should have trusted his impulsiveness.

"Blackbird" played in his head as they motored up the Santa Monica Freeway toward Fort Ord. Michael leaned forward, catching a thin scrim of sunshine falling over the seat in front of him. Warm and flowing across his cheeks and neck. He cherished its purity. He vowed to try to never forget the feeling.

iv.

EVEN HIDING in the bedroom with Julieta cannot shut it out. When he lays in bed, a folded pillow propped under his neck, staring at the blank wall, Tom sees dead soldiers being dragged through the mud of Vietnam, he sees students being gunned down on college campuses, he sees young people clubbed by cops in the street, he sees Black Panthers murdered in their homes, missing children, houses on fire, brutal murders in the hills. It goes on and on and on. It's as though everything from the TV news has been implanted in his eyes. When he closes them, he hears people suffering, he hears the moaning of friends who've taken too many drugs, he hears the wailing of the poor, of the sick, of the hungry. It goes on and on and on.

And then one night he and Julieta became one among them, wounded and bleeding in the Hollywood Hills from the aftermath, shivering and traumatized, awaiting their rescue. Blood trickled down his forehead. Bruises bloomed on her forearms.

If he dwells too long, Tom will relive all his doubts, the little voices that whispered not to go, that it was stupid to make a buy from strangers in the middle of nowhere in the middle of the night. A hackneyed setup right out of a second-rate script.

Such is the outcome when you find you've become part of the story: You hide in the bedroom. When your girlfriend's pain becomes too much to handle, you escape to the bathroom. Back and forth all day long.

He needs a way out. This is no way to lead a life.

"They are our friends," Julieta insists. She's on her back, eyes closed, a bare leg poking out of the blanket. One arm hugs a pillow, the other reaches backward, her fingers dragging along the brass slats of the headboard.

She says, "They understand."

And it is true, they all are close friends, perhaps the only ones who genuinely are friends of both the boy's mom *and* the actor. The couple first met the actor through Julieta's TV dubbing work for *Looney Tunes*, and then through Tom they met the boy's mom at UCLA. Soon, they were a group. A team. Inseparable.

Tom wonders about such an assumption. "Right," he says. "But we've never asked."

"Friends don't have to ask. Friends *know*."

The curtains remain drawn, holding in a strange odor of habitation. A single beam of early morning sunshine trails down the sill. The room feels less like it's shuttered and more as if it's nighttime.

"Julieta," he begins. His voice is low and quiet. He can hear the boy tiptoeing in the next room, getting ready for school. The truth is that Tom is just as freaked out as Julieta about reengaging with the world. Terrified that every event in his until now unremarkable life eventually will run into violence. That any interaction is charged. But he also knows how easy it would be to resign to a permanent state of retreat. And that idea is even more terrifying.

Something needs to change.

He tells Julieta that they'll need to go back to their apartment. They can't hide out in this bedroom forever, plus they're putting their friend out on the couch. And, he notes, they need to think about the boy. How he might be taking this. We need a plan, he advises.

"We have to find some strength to get our strength back."

She reminds him of that time they saw a wounded cat on the neighbor's yard, how it looked so helpless, how it looked as though it wanted comfort and attention, but when they stepped toward it on the lawn, the cat found the strength to stand up, arch its back, and hiss at them.

He says, "We can't live like that. Or like this."

She says, "They are our friends."

Walking up South Oakhurst, Tom imagines the duplex behind him like a balloon on a string that he's towing as it floats higher and higher into the sky. Being outside makes him that much lighter, he must admit, a break from being confined in the nervous terror that he and Julieta have managed to create.

He's left her there to sleep in the otherwise empty house. It's only a matter of minutes. A test to see if he can make it as far as the Rexall across the intersection of Pico. If he has the wherewithal to function without panic. She'll be safe alone in the duplex. After all, across the street is the semi-modern apartment building that is reputed to house the legendary Lakers superstar guard, Jerry West.

Slow and off-kilter, Tom steps over a long pink worm nestled in a sidewalk crack. The air is fresh, the sun tempered by a light breeze. He smiles at a woman sitting in a station wagon idling under the shade of an Indian laurel tree. Finding his step, he kicks a stray bottle cap from one sidewalk square to the next. It's peaceful. He thinks he can make it. Behind the plate glass windows of the bungalows and the minimal traditionals lining the street, retired men and women watch him from the shadows of their living rooms. One even waves.

Ahead, he can see the giant intersection of West Pico populated with a blush and bevy of foot commuters crowding the sidewalk, waiting for the light to change, teetering off the pavement's edge, ready to be first to cross the heavily trafficked boulevard. A raw energy that is beautiful and inspiring. Directly across West Pico, the Rexall Drugs anchors the corner, its iconic orange logo and lights beaming as though permanently caught in sunset, that place where movie stars had been discovered, or so someone said.

He can do it.

The sound of Julieta's voice spirals down the block, somewhere between plaintive and betrayed. He turns around quickly, at first pretending not to see her standing on the stoop in an oversized terrycloth robe she found in the closet. Then he looks to one of the neighbors watching him through a window. The line of his imaginary balloon has gone slack.

Tom just wants to reach the Rexall. That's all he needs.

Julieta continues to call after him, her timbre half in the tone of one of her *Looney Tunes* voices, an occasional Spanish word flying out.

Deep down he knows this is nothing more than a mythical monster created out of their collective fear. That's all it is. Throughout the county there are seven million people spread over thousands of square miles. As impossible as it might seem to disappear under the eyes of so many people, for the life of them, they have still managed to feel as though they are the most vulnerable ones on the face of the earth. This is no way to live. These aren't dark and deserted streets. This is Los Angeles.

They shouldn't have to worry, and yet they do. It can happen to anyone, these bad things.

She begs him to hurry. Please. *Por favor.*

But for the moment he can't go any direction. He doesn't know what to do. Tom just stands there, fingering the deep scratches on his face, gazing at the woman in the station wagon as she drives off into the orange glow of the Rexall, leaving behind a curl of exhaust. He can't keep feeding the monster, and yet he can't leave Julieta to suffer it alone. Wait and wait and wait. What else can he do? For the moment they both are safe. As long as no one moves. Wait and wait and wait. Knowing that at least he is in full view of the semi-modern apartment building across the street, the one in which Jerry West supposedly lives, where from whichever unit is his he can see Tom *and* Julieta out his front window, a confirmation and relief that nothing bad can happen under the watchful eye of a legendary guard.

The End

i.

ALTHOUGH SHE keeps a little apartment in town, Billie spends most of her days in an abandoned condo at the coastal redwood village. It sits at the far end of the original gated development, waiting to be demolished when the weather turns. The once stylish early '70s complex, built as an eco-community, will be reborn as luxury condos that complement the more recent construction on the property. "*Traditional Modern*," the developers advertise on a giant sign at the head of the path. "*The Future Never Seemed More Familiar*." It's illustrated with a schematic of the landscaping, as well as sample floor plans of each forthcoming dwelling. This is the second such sign. The first was replaced after it was defaced with a giant circle with a slash through the middle, made with spray paint.

Initially, Billie lugged up two boxes of books and magazines into the empty apartment. Then she snuck in a rolled-up futon and blanket for comfort. And when Billie discovered there was power, she brought over an electric tea kettle, a box of tea bags, and two mugs. She alternates them.

Neither a trespasser nor a violator. Instead, in a way, a caretaker.

Over the past three months, she's learned the pattern of the condo village, knowing when she can come and when she can go. She arrives at about 8:30, between the early walkers and mid-morning strollers. Reclined on the futon on the floor and leaned against the living room wall, Billie spends most days reading, only looking up to gaze out the window when the fog drifts between the two giant redwoods that form a gateway into the bluffs that overlook the Pacific. When she does leave for her apartment in town (before dark, as it would be too risky to turn on the condo lights), she'll wander along the fence that lines the cliffs, a slow walk that she counts as exercise, looking out at the waves splashing over the rocks and into the seawall, listening to seals bark.

She first came in through an open window. Now she keeps the front door unlocked. No one seems to notice.

The end of her marriage took the best out of her. Kind of killed her that it came so late in life, which is why when the subject comes up, she refers to Howard as *The Widower*.

This Tuesday morning, in the empty space between New Year's and Easter, she arrives at the abandoned condo at the usual time. In town it was sunny, but only for thirty minutes or so until the fog rolled off the ocean. It's amazing how quickly the fog can sweep in, suddenly extinguishing the sunlight; and yet once it arrives, the fog can linger forever, as though there is no possible path out.

It's part of what drew her here to the north coast.

She turns the front door handle, greeted by the scents of her teas and used books. Looking both ways to ensure she's not seen, Billie slips through the cracked open door and then quickly closes it, nearly stepping on a pink sheet of paper pushed up against the bottom stair. A standard size photocopy, with the intrusiveness of a home invader.

Slipping on her reading glasses, Billie kneels down. She doesn't want to touch the paper. In a bland yet formal font, the announcement on the pink photocopy reads:

Calling All Residents!
The Future Never Seemed More Familiar = Profit Before Principles
<u>Save the Founding Ideals of Our Community.</u>
Meeting: Wednesday, 1:00 p.m. Community Center.

While she is slightly relieved at the generic nature of the flyer, what Billie can't figure out is why it was slipped under her door sometime in the night, that of an abandoned building.

In her own way, she supposes, maybe she is a part of this community.

She remembers the feeling when she arrived on their very first visit to the north coast. Like returning to a long-lost home. Billie might have even said that to Howard. *Returning home.* That was thirty years ago. Over that time, they took so many subsequent vacations to the redwood community that they started to recognize faces. She imagined eventually they'd end up there permanently. She imagined many things.

The Community Center is swelling. Near the front door, to the left, residents slip out of wet ponchos and raincoats, hanging them above the growing collection of umbrellas, some shoved into a metal vase and others sprawled around it, left open to dry. Each time the door opens, Billie can hear the rain pounding. It smells briny, of the ocean's surface.

The volume of the chatter is startling. Almost ritualistic, it reminds her of cicadas singing from the grasses at dusk. She stands just inside the entrance, her jacket unzipped, an old-fashioned yellow slicker that makes her feel somewhere between a fisherman and a yield sign. A few of the residents look familiar. These are the people Howard would have called "our people."

It's a risk being here, Billie knows. This isn't her event, and she so easily could get caught. She really shouldn't have come. But each time she stepped over that flyer at the bottom of the stairs, she kept thinking it was no accident that it had been left there. For two days, she told herself to ignore the feeling. But the next thing she knew, she was marching in the rain behind a small stream of residents on the path toward the Community Center. In general, she's been trying to be less impulsive. More deliberate. And that's one thing she can't blame on Howard. It's been her whole life.

A woman about her age walks right up to her. And, as if sent to prove Howard right, she looks like someone Billie would know: close-cropped silver hair, a poncho sweater with southwestern patterns, and loose jeans tucked into roughed-up brown leather boots.

"Thanks for coming," she says to Billie, without introducing herself. She carries herself as though Billie should know her.

"Please, take off your jacket. Stay."

Then the woman marches to the center of the room, taking her place in front of a round table. She coughs several times, trying to get people's attention. A man in the far corner puts two fingers to his lips and blows what sounds like a factory whistle, quieting the room.

Someone says, "Thank you, Gary. . . . The floor is yours now, Cassandra."

Billie keeps her jacket on.

Cassandra clasps her hands, drawing them over her heart. She says she's warmed by how many people came out today. And on such a lousy afternoon. It only shows what they've known all along: this community is special. One whose original founders saw it as a beacon of social commitment, of kindness, of real community, and of an appreciation of Mother Earth herself. But now she needs us, our community. Everyone here needs to stand up and tell the developers that we don't support the new building plans. That we don't want our community transformed into luxury villas. It was founded on values. And, she adds, don't be fooled by their buzz words of *renewables* and *sustainability* and *zero-carbon*. Those are nothing but focus-grouped, mythmaking selling points.

It makes Billie think of Howard. How quickly he transformed his international consulting business on clean air initiatives into promoting multinational corporate trade policies, trying to claim he could accomplish more for social equity by being on the inside. It seemed he mostly got rich.

Petitions are scattered atop the round table behind Cassandra. Ballpoint pens set beside each clipboard. And Cassandra is looking for members with expertise to join various task forces, such as reviewing all the permits and contracts, communicating with the media, working with the town and the county to find any regulations concerning zoning, and further inquiry into a lawsuit by the current owners based on breach of contract regarding the expectations each resident had about the community in making their purchase.

All this talk draws Billie back almost fifty years, to Peter Rubin's backyard on Airdrome Drive when she and other students were trying to stop America's violence in Southeast Asia by forming SEWN. But with distance and reflection, she also is aware of the potential for failure. In the end, they'd done nothing, caught in the same circular currents as everyone else.

Ironically, she has no stake in the fight to preserve the values of this cherished redwood community, other than being a long-time guest, a dreamer who had to compromise for a cramped apartment in town because Howard gave up on them in the home stretch. And yet she is compelled to action. What she is witnessing here in the Community Center confirms that she still despises bureaucracy and that, at best, it only works for the long haul. But this is urgent. There are demolition dates being set. Once the bulldozers and the dumpsters show up, then it is a fait accompli, after which all the committees in the world won't matter other than to commiserate and share their grief, and probably secretly relish the rise in value of their own properties.

Shaking her head, Billie looks around at everyone signing up for committees and perusing the petitions on the table as though they're bidding in a long-term silent auction.

All these people in here. How is it that she, Billie, can be the one who is most willing to wage the battle, to put up the fight?

These are not "our" people.

These people are staging their fight with jargon and slogans and plans that are less about protecting this one-time sanctuary and more about assuaging their own guilt over their privilege and their success. They are, in fact, the target audience of the developers.

She pinches her zipper, carefully sliding the pull between the teeth to keep it from catching the fabric.

When Billie was twenty-two, she watched an actor on a talk show humbly discuss all the accolades and awards he'd received for his blockbuster adaptation of a book everyone had seemed to love. He was the son of a movie legend who her parents adored, but she recognized him as the strangely familiar man from the airplane when she'd left the country. She decided to send him a letter, saying she'd sat next to him on a flight to Berlin, that it was a crazy flight during a crazy, frightening, and awful time, being persecuted by the government and, basically, being driven out of the country. She mostly wanted the actor to know that she remembered the book he was reading, and it inspired her to read it too, and later she too counted herself as among those who loved it—in fact, the book had gotten her through some of the worst of it. Now she couldn't wait to see his award-winning film. She just wanted him to know. When a reply came some months later, stuck upside down inside the envelope was a signed headshot and a note from the actor's publicist saying that the actor appreciated the devotion, and that he had included the requested autograph. Howard teased her about keeping it for all these years. During dinner parties he'd send her to the hall closet to pull the picture out. He'd make her tell the story over and over and again while he sat braced on his chair for the punchline, and there was nothing she could do but try to be a good sport and laugh along.

Six weeks after the meeting in the Community Center, Billie stares down the demolition crew from the condo window. There have been no more flyers left under her door. No other public displays. And even in town she hasn't heard any talk about stopping the project.

Chained and locked, she is ready. Her bright yellow raincoat ensures she'll be seen.

She glares at the startled bulldozer operators. At the men leaned against the wrecking ball, shaking their heads and talking on cell phones. She tries to figure out the "anti" crowd who gather behind the yellow tape, apparently not to protest but to gawk, many of them aiming their phones up at her for pictures. This has taken them by complete surprise. There is no reason for anyone down there to expect that someone would be inside, much less shackled to a support beam near the front window.

Each time she shifts, the chains tug on her wrists. Chafe against her ribs.

When Billie really thinks about it, the condo is worn down and outdated. A boxy living room, and to the right a small dining area abutting a kitchen with dark brown stained cabinets and tan laminate countertops. Straight through the living room are two bedrooms separated by a small bathroom. The walls are thin, white plasterboard, and you can see the roller streaks and a small stucco patch covering an accidental hole that the bedroom doorknob put through the wall. There is low-pile brown carpet everywhere except in the kitchen and the bathroom (matching the laminate on the countertops), and on bare feet it feels a little sticky—maybe due to the chemical treatments that were meant to help it last longer.

It is hard to justify its saving. She knows that. But preservation is not just about the object or the structure. It is also about ideals, ones that can't just be rebuilt because once demolished, they are gone forever.

The redwoods. The sounds of the wind. The tenacity of sunlight cutting through the fog. And the smell of the ocean. *Home.* She is ready. Prepared for what, she doesn't know.

Billie holds steady, watching the crowd grow. Sirens spin and wail in the distance. Everyone keeps watching her. She wants them to see her as an activist. Not as some kind of performance artist in her yellow slicker, arms open wide and dangling chains. Beside the foreman, Cassandra looks up at her, squinting, a hand pressed against her forehead. It's impossible to tell if she is saluting or just shading her eyes.

ii.

IN the woods outside of Canmore, Albie Thompson has been watching a fox die. It's been almost a week now. The listless fox, no bigger than a large house cat, is nestled in a cluster of brush, off the trail along the Bow River, under the watch of the Three Sisters peaks. Just a stone's throw away is Main Street, the town's city center, full of life, a shopping area that still feels like it's out of Canada's western past of cowboys and railroad towns. In eight years of walking these trails since he absconded to the Canadian Rockies, an area known for its wildlife, this week was the first time Albie ever saw a fox. And each day has seemed as though it might be the last. But she's always there the next morning, still alive and waiting. He calls her the Miracle Fox.

Following a morning of packing his suitcase to be ready for to-morrow's departure, Albie heads out for the trail, on this, his last full day in Canmore.

The fox is lying on her side, head flat against the ground. She looks smaller than yesterday. Thinner. Her ribs bow with each breath. Albie stands a few feet back. Tufts of fur blow off her body with the slightest breeze, revealing glassy sores. Looking down with uncertain authority, Albie pats his coat pocket to feel for the stick of jerky he's tucked inside a paper napkin. The routine be-came to feed the fox as he was leaving, tearing the beef in half, tossing one part by her head, and keeping the other for himself. He's tried to eat with her, but she won't touch hers until he leaves.

"And how is Miracle Fox today?" Albie asks. "Feeling stronger, I hope?" Albie believes in the power of keeping positive. Of rein-forcing hope to clear away obstructed paths.

On other days, the fox's eyes have gazed toward Albie when he speaks. But now they're fixed on something in the distance, fogged and unchanged except for an occasional blink to wipe away a bug.

Albie leans in a little. "I have some news to share. Maybe even some good news."

The fox's eyes don't move.

Albie kneels down until he's almost eye level, but keeping out of striking distance. He fingers a pine cone, rolling it around before mindlessly picking it up.

"It's okay just to listen," he says. "One doesn't always have to respond." He tosses the pine cone into the bushes, but it ricochets off a branch and drops down near the fox's head, landing between her snout and her ear, the one that's folded down.

"This came yesterday." Albie reaches into the breast pocket of his button-up and shakes open a letter, one that's been unfolded and refolded so many times that already it looks about to separate into four perfect quarters. Right down the middle is the White House logo.

"Now listen up," he tells the fox. "This is big."

Albie proceeds to read aloud President Carter's proclamation that was issued on his first day of office, a pardon offering amnesty to draft evaders. The letter is personalized, addressed to his real name, not his pseudonym. It seems they knew where he was all along.

"So what does that mean, you might ask," he says. "It means that I'm going home."

The fox's body jerks. Without moving her head, she manages a weak growl, trying to bare her teeth. They both want to feel the joy of revival.

The next morning, two hours before he needs to be at the bus station, Albie makes one last walk to feed the fox. Hands pulled behind his back, he grips a ragged bouquet of wildflowers picked along the way. He'll leave them with her. All living creatures are owed their measure of dignity.

It hadn't been too strange to be in a suddenly empty apartment. The truth is, he could barely remember ever having lived there. Since he escaped to this little town in Alberta, he always willed the situation to be temporary, and as such, he never made the flat into a home, only a functional space. In fact, he'd kept the same suitcase that he arrived with in the corner of the living room, visible and ready to be packed, an intimate companion, the corners battered, the blue vinyl well faded. Once, on a whim, coming home from a bartending gig he'd taken during summer tourist season, he bought a bunch of flowers, something he thought would breathe life into the flat. He ended up sneezing all night.

At the usual cluster, the fox's body is gone. Only a small nest of twigs and leaves, slightly ruffled, give an indication that she once lie there. He's always heard that animals crawl off when they're ready to die. (Didn't the fox already do that once? Isn't that how she ended up in in this spot the first place?) But now, staring at the abandoned space with almost no traces of the fox's form, he imagines it can be the opposite, too.

Either way, it does kind of break his heart, the parting.

She really is a miracle fox.

He tosses the last stick of jerky into the bushes, believing she'll find it once he's gone. And then, still clutching the flowers he intended to leave, Albie turns around and walks toward town. Back to his soon-to-be abandoned apartment. But the wildflowers won't go to waste. He'll leave the bouquet in the flat for the next tenants, hoping they aren't allergic.

Here, for eight years, Alban Thompson was called Percy Roth, living a nearly monastic life in order not to bring attention to himself. It must have worked. No one ever really knew he existed. And, strange as it is, they never will.

Traipsing down 8th Street, Albie is light on his feet. Brought back to life and already in celebration of the miracles of absolution.

iii.

AT AN opening on Pico, three blocks before the next stoplight when the traffic always backs up endlessly, the boy's mom guns the engine of the 356, and the car starts to soar weightless, a world without gravity, limitless and free. She cuts the radio, draws and holds her breath, shuts down all forms of communication because this is the place, this is a space of purity in motion, where body and machinery and laws of physics are indistinguishable.

They know to inhale the fresh air. Take it in while they can. Great-grandmother's apartment will be tainted with a shut-in smell, it always is, windows rarely opened, cooking oils appropriated into the walls.

Together, under a mid-morning sunlight that is sharp and welcoming, they blaze over L.A. streets. Just barely skirting the earth, a world for only the two of them.

The actor was the first to get a Porsche, a blue one, after he'd made a movie about a freewheeling guy who drove a Porsche 356 up and down the PCH; as part of his contract, the cash-strapped producers gave him the car at the end of the shoot. After having zoomed around in the actor's Porsche, the boy's mom also wanted one. Such desire was uncharacteristic of her, since she, a schoolteacher, usually didn't go for such things. And yet one afternoon on the way home from her classroom in East L.A., she stopped and traded in her iconic blue VW bus for a gold 356 built the year after her son was born. To her, a sporty car like that symbolized youthful freedom, not wealth. She understood the potential.

Soon they are crawling through the intersection. After the boy's mom turns back up the radio, they hear the DJ on KHJ Boss Radio announce that next up is a song off Paul McCartney's first solo album. The one, he says, we've all been waiting for. The one everybody's been talking about.

The boy scoots to the edge of the passenger's seat. He didn't know there was a solo album. That there was one everybody's been talking about. He leans forward until his head is in line with the bottom of the door, his ear nearly against the speaker.

Wow. Imagine that: Paul McCartney without The Beatles.

He hears a slow wandering along the piano keys before the chords turn confident, and the voice that the boy knows so well drops in with *"Maybe I'm amazed at the way you love me all the time."*

This is exhilaration, and this is disloyalty.

Curiously loose, the song is a little homespun. And yet Paul hasn't abandoned the sound of The Beatles. There but not quite: the guitar solo something George would play but a little more Paul, exchanging gentle vulnerability for more deliberate and vocalized notes; the backing vocals familiar and new at once; the whole song sounding like an old recipe with slightly altered ingredients, but it still boils, steams, and intoxicates.

While the boy doesn't know the words or where it's going, he wants to sing along because the boy feels like the song is coming from inside of him, a quaking inside his chest as though it's his song and it's him making it come alive through the radio.

And thus, the betrayal. It's as if McCartney is saying he doesn't need The Beatles anymore, and fool that the boy is, he's buying into it—because that song sounds so good and so alive, and the boy knows that this is something he could live with forever. Even his mom hums along with the backing *ahs*. She who saw The Beatles in Dodger Stadium just four years earlier and complained of the screaming and of the setlist that ignored the innovations of *Revolver* and *Rubber Soul*, she too is part of the betrayal.

The boy only is ten years old, and some in his family worry that he's become too accustomed to unsteadiness and unpredictability. A mother who has been divorced since before the boy can remember. A father so far out of his life that even the idea of him having any biological connection to the boy is so wholly unimaginable that it seems more likely that he descended from a rib. But it is a normal life he leads. His mother is there to sing to him when he wakes up. She's there to hold and kiss him when he goes to sleep. And in spite of whatever comes next in an unsteady world, that sense of steadiness is something he knows can always be counted on.

The song roars on as they continue to eke their way along Beverly Boulevard, passing drug stores and clothiers and small groceries and Mount Sinai Hospital, where his grandfather makes his rounds. When for no noticeable reason the street clears, the boy's mom pushes the car into a higher gear, and for just a moment it feels like they are flying again.

It's joyous—the speed, the song, the freedom.

Once on Fairfax Avenue, the boy's mom slows down and pulls into a space right in front of Great-grandmother's apartment building. It's as though it was waiting for them. She leaves the car running while the song winds down in the slow piano movement with which it began.

Listening, the boy gazes out the window into his great-grand-mother's first-floor kitchen. Everyone else already is there as they are every weekend. A West Coast settlement for Brooklyn refugees. Milling around the countertops and the stove, they are talking and picking at the food, their huge faces, flopping ears, magnificent smiles, and giant eyebrows. Glamorous, comical, beautiful, and frightening.

His mom says, "That was a pretty good song, don't you think?"

The boy wants to be dismissive. Judgmental. Note the flaws. Be the one to specify exactly why Paul needs John, and that without him there is no *solo*, just a missing half.

Instead, he says what he's really thinking; he tells her, "I hope they play it again when we drive home."

They look at each other, and then the boy's mom leans across the stick shift, lays both hands on his face and kisses his forehead.

"Time for us to go in," she says.

This is their life. The two of them making their way through the world.

iv.

THE WOMAN who had become my wife got sick. Not sick, but ill. She woke up one morning, pressed a hand on her belly that was hard as a rock, turned to me, and said, "I'm a goner."

We were getting along in years. But not that far along.

I made appointments. Scheduled consults and tests. She knew I wasn't equipped to deal with this. To get through it, I needed a job. I became our project manager: planning, arranging, and advocating. She went along with this on my behalf. You had to admire her.

She endured a lot. Surgeries that were called exploratory but were in fact as invasive and debilitating as any major procedure. Endless blood tests. Samples of every other kind of fluid. Her body humiliated in every possible way. And in the end, it all pointed right back to her belly, just as she'd diagnosed. Only now it was named.

You could tell her main doctor, the oncologist at the university hospital center, also was thinking *goner*. In an exam room, we sat in the plastic chairs while he sat on top of the examination table. His legs dangled. We literally had to look up to him. A pile of folders, placed neatly beside him on the paper bedsheet, kept slipping when he took his hand off the pile.

With the test results evaluated by a faceless board of colleagues, he mulled the outcomes in his head. We waited in silence. It looked as if he was doing math, carrying remainders from one imaginary column to the next.

He opened with saying he prided himself on being realistic. No one, the doctor said, was ready to throw in the towel.

He spoke with an accent, one we would talk about endlessly, trying to place. We settled on Balkan, in its most general sense, in part due to his high forehead and symmetrical jet-black hairline that we recognized from a professional tennis player who was from the region. That doctor was a real mystery, with a curious mix of compassion and absolute authority. Before he'd come in, his nurse told us we were lucky. He was the best, she wanted us to know, the leading researcher in the world on what the woman who had become my wife was presenting. Her endorsement was unprompted and meant to be reassuring. But you could hear the way she lingered on the word *lucky*.

Moving one of the folders to his lap and opening it up, the doctor talked in percentages that would make most people fall apart. But given that we saw our baseline as zero, each number looked like a small gift. Fine jewelry, I thought, comes in small boxes. He prescribed a whole regiment of drugs and treatments. And in case it wasn't understood, the doctor again reiterated the percentages, which he made clear were based solely on aggregate data and statistics. As for the individual, well, it was difficult to make any predictions.

The woman who had become my wife caught my eye. She dragged her index finger across her throat.

Drugs were layered over other drugs. Each one to mitigate the effects of the one that came before it. The whole thing was circular in a way that seemed to have no end. At least not of the type we wanted to reach. On unexpected occasions, a certain combination lifted her right out of this world. Took her straight into an alternate reality, nearly fading or dissolving the room, but from which she always came back feeling more at peace, as though that was where the good parts of life were. It was hard not to be envious.

Reclining in the infusion chair at the university hospital, she stared out into space. It was a routine for us but not yet a habit. Soft music played in the background, mostly songs from our youth now meant to inspire relaxation. It was impossible to imagine that they once had signified rebellion. Now they were part of the blah, blah, blah of the everyday world.

I sat beside her. A magazine spread across my lap. As if it would ever get read.

The oncological nurse walked an older man to his infusion chair in the opposite corner of the room. Passing in front of us with a slow waddle, he led with his right arm, lifted and bent; in the crook, a tattered remnant of gauze from a blood draw. The nurse helped him into his chair, reciting instructions and procedures and reassurances. She looked tired of him.

He kept gazing my way. He really wanted to talk. To connect. And who could blame him. He looked utterly unprepared for any of this.

I felt lousy for ignoring him, but I had my loyalties, my respon-
sibilities, and as much it killed me to think it, I just couldn't be
god's social worker.

But then he blurted out how this was his first time here. Announced it, like a bugle pointed at the ceiling. The nurse shook
her head. She stepped between us—me, the woman who had
become my wife, and the man.

That nurse knew what was coming next.

Speaking around her, the man added that he meant as a patient. He said he was no stranger here. He'd had three friends
who'd come to this center for treatment over the years. This very
room. He'd visited each of them more than once. Sat with them.
"They're all dead now."

The nurse just stood there as though trying to smother a fire.

I looked down at the floor, a pleasant pattern of carpet squares.
It was impossible to see the seams. You wondered how it all fit
together.

She lifted her arm, the woman who had become my wife, and
pointed a crooked index finger at me. The IV tube followed behind in obedience. She rolled her head to the side, facing me. Her
eyelids were red. A slightly glassy stare. She whispered, "All of
this, and you still don't have any jokes?"

When they lowered her casket into the grave, the two young
men dangling the rope on each end got their signals crossed.
The box swung right to left, at one point knocking against the
dirt sidewalls. They slowly pulled the casket up and worked the
snag out of the rope. Then the box went up and down in short
bursts. We were standing around it, the freshly dug hole, on a
hill overlooking a valley. Maybe only twenty of us, although
who was counting. You could tell no one knew whether to watch
this sideshow or to look away for a moment, in order to take
the pressure off the two young cemetery workers. I'd found the
whole day agonizing, was not able to absorb much. Being there
was more like something you would imagine, not actually experience. The guy at the far end nodded to his partner one-two-

three, and he pulled up. The casket tilted on the head side as though taking a forward bow.

Her brother smiled to himself and muttered, "She would have loved this."

For days after the treatments, she'd sing one of the random songs we'd heard at the clinic. One would manage to worm its way in, lodge into her head, and stick throughout the week. At home, it would just slip out. And you never knew when. Padding her way down the hallway to the living room. From her bed. In the bath. Once she hummed one of the tunes in her sleep in the middle of the night. She hated it. She said it was a form of mind control, implanted her brain. These once meaningful songs had turned villainous. Antagonistic.

She said, "It's like a leash from the medical establishment, making sure I remember that I'm reliant on them."

The treatments left her lousy with sicknesses that she could only describe as being like the flu, but, she'd say, like a flu you never had or would ever want to have. It would go on for three days, and all the while she'd question whether to go in again. After one day or so of relief, she'd get just enough strength back to keep moving forward. That was the pattern. You couldn't pretend otherwise.

This week's lingering song was "Here Comes the Sun." And, different from the rest, this time it wasn't driving her nuts. She wasn't pretending to hit the side of her head as if to knock it out. Instead, she was gloriously singing it. No longer just a remnant soundtrack, the song was like a benediction of life, a refrain that broke up an endless day into parts, in which each section felt like a new and glorious beginning, the kind of place you couldn't even imagine leaving, which made me infinitely sad in a way I had to keep to myself.

In the living room, she stood in front of the window, totally enveloped by the sunshine, singing the song aloud. She was wearing her white nightgown, a thin summer cotton, translucent, and yet no sense of a physical form beneath it. No outline of a body.

Or legs or hips or arms or bones or breasts. It was just single radiance.

For at least a half hour she stood there.

Then she stopped singing and turned to me. For the first time in months, her expression commanded strength and confidence.

And then she said, "Maybe *we* are the tear in the fabric."

I wasn't sure what that meant.

She said, "When they vandalized the billboard, the Paul Mc-Cartney head." She reminded me that she'd described it as a tear in our cultural fabric, and I'd proposed that she was only seeing the spaces between an already torn up world.

"Did I really say that?"

"And you said how it was the space between the tears that let in the light."

"That part does sound like me." I wished I could remember it better.

"Does it ever. . . . And yet, look at us." She turned and was washed over again by the sun. For a moment I thought she was gone. I had to blink.

ACKNOWLEDGMENTS

Much appreciation to: the UNO team of GK, Abram, Chelsey, Katie, and Alex for all they have done to help this book along; Alisson and Addison for unconditional love, both given and taken; my writing family that has gathered every year for almost two decades at the dinner table of Robert and Peg Boyers, forever inspiring and motivating; and especially Rick, who was there to help pry away the doubt.